EQUINOX

EQUINOX

MADHURI MAITRA

PARTRIDGE
A Penguin Random House Company

To order additional copies of this book, contact
Partridge India
000 800 10062 62
orders.india@partridgepublishing.com

www.partridgepublishing.com/india

dedicated to

the stylus

and

the quill

Acknowledgements

Moupia Basu,

for that crucial first editing

Rajoshree Maitra,

for her elegant cover design

family and friends

He rushed into the shack to escape the sudden torrent, cursing that he had left his umbrella behind. Who would believe he was a local of Allepey? Or, should he say Alapuzha? No Malayali worth his fish and rice would forget his umbrella; he would carry it around like a fifth limb in the month of June, the official harbinger of the Indian monsoon. He shook his thick curly mop of hair, lost a few drops of rain to the muddy floor of the shack. He wished he could do the same to his beard! He shook out the white lungi, his preferred mode of dressing, when he was holidaying at home.

'One tea, please', he indicated to the lungi-clad lad behind the table and settled himself on an old wooden bench. Ignoring the curious glances of the other patrons, gossiping in groups before heading out to their respective jobs, he flipped open his laptop and began browsing.

Kerala is the one state in India that boasts 100 percent literacy. Those were the statistics of a long time ago; no doubt they were still true. Deeply rooted in their culture and language, Keralites were as comfortable with English as with Malayali. They had a sharp business acumen; men and women alike were happy to travel far and wide for good careers.

Kerala is a small state, roughly 38,000 square kilometres, its peculiar elongated shape lines a portion of India's western coast. Human habitation spills over onto the highways, its population as dense as its vegetation once was. There are about nine national highways that criss-cross it at different points—the inevitable urban development. There's barely a vacant space in the state. The still lush, green state draws its own share of domestic and foreign tourists. Kerala's USP is its Ayurvedic spas—state-of-the-art fusions of the modern and the traditional. And when the patrons, people from all over the world, were not enjoying the body and soul services of these dispensers of wellness, they were logged into their countries, jobs, emails, spouses and paramours.

Johny Kutty's browser went indecisively from one tab to the next. He checked his mail. Someone had sent him a link to some story competition. Johny clicked without interest. Fiction was not the forte of the Rambler (his famous professional pseudonym). He was a rolling stone, a rambler, uncharacteristically stationed in his native Alapuzha, in Kerala for 15 days (*or longer, if necessary*, Chettan had sternly insisted—*property disputes took some time*). He needed to travel, and to write. It was his lifeblood.

Equinox. Well, ohh . . . kay! Short story . . . blah-blah-blah . . . to be submitted by September 22, the autumnal equinox. (Rambler rolled his eyes upward—how pompous these publishers sounded!) Fiction! He could try it! And then, there was the prize money, 2,00,000 INR. No treasure chest, this, but not chicken feed either.

I could use it. It would be something to do while he waited for the property papers to be ready.

It was just the end of June. He had two months, almost three. Piece of cake! Rambler stretched out his legs and leaned against a tree, part of the decor of the shack. The matted roof was simply built around this grand old palm. Magically, the lungi-clad lad appeared before him, sure of a larger order from the relaxed gent. Three minutes later, Rambler was tucking into soft, hot idlis, having his second cup of tea and playing with ideas. The rain drummed steadily on.

* *

It was also raining in Mumbai, further up the coast. Ruchi Sharma stared at the downpour from her one-bedroom flat in Vashi, a growing suburb of Mumbai. Vashi was a hobo compared to its sophisticated metropolitan cousin Mumbai, but she loved it here. She had grown up in the suburb and been the head girl of St Agnes's. That same one-bedroom flat—301, Meera Apartments, Phase II—had seen her born, grow tall, attain puberty, top school, not top college, get her first miserable little cell phone. It had witnessed her fights with her father when her boyfriend Sanjay Gupta bought her a nicer cell phone than her father could afford. It was where she sat now, watching the rain longingly, as she thought of what she should do next.

College was over—that is to say, she had graduated with a bachelor's degree in English literature, and that was the extent to which her father could educate her. He was not mean or autocratic—just a regular middle-class guy with modest values and a modest income. He'd given his daughter the best education he could; his wife now needed the money to get together Ruchi's trousseau (*the wretched girl has such expensive tastes*, she would often complain. And this was blamed on the cosmopolitan influence of Mumbai). They thought it would be wise for Ruchi to marry a Mumbai boy, one who would understand the problems and aspirations of a girl raised here. No one in their native Jalandhar would put up with Ruchi's nakhras. And anyway, their son Rajeev was the horse they were backing. Sons were supposed to look after the parents when they grew old. Therefore, Rajeev had to be educated well and given all encouragement, so that he could take the family's fortunes higher than the third-floor one-bedroom flat.

The living room, which also doubled as Ruchi's and Rajeev's bedroom, overlooked the main roads crossing below. There was a fountain, which was turned on in the late afternoon and turned off again at 10 p.m. No one turned it on during the furious monsoon. Ruchi stared at the fountain and prayed for something interesting to happen to her. She had applied for a job at a women's garment showroom in the Vashi market, much to her parents' disapproval. What was the use of her education, they had thundered. To appease them, Ruchi was tutoring her neighbour's six-year-old in spoken English—a difficult task, since the only words he ever grasped were 'bowling' (which he pronounced 'balling') and 'batting'. He was only too happy to have the tuition cancelled, as today; Ruchi had to go out to meet Sanjay. Luckily for Ruchi, the neighbour was a gullible sort. She had handed over the full tuition fee with very little fuss because Ruchi promised to make up the loss of any cancelled classes; but really, she lost no sleep over this increasing heap of cancelled classes.

Her cell phone rang just as she had donned her best pair of jeans and top (she would change into the really sexy one in her bag at the washroom in the mall before she met Sanjay). It was Kavita, her friend from St Angelo's. Kavita D'Sa was as nerdy as Ruchi was glamour-struck, but they both had remained staunch friends since primary school.

'Ruchi, do you want to write?' Kavita squealed, excited.

And Ruchi, ever adventurous, thought, *Why not?* It was not a possibility she had explored but—why not?

'OK, Kavi, write for what? A magazine?' Ruchi had immediate visions of herself in the beautiful office of the *Starry Skies* magazine, creating and writing gossip about film stars. Even Shobhaa De had begun there, she recalled inaccurately.

'No, no, it's a story competition. A short story competition. Anyone over eighteen can participate. You have to be an Indian citizen. Write a short story of up to 3,000 words and submit it by September 22. That is the autumnal equinox.'

Trust Kavi to remember boring stuff like that. Ruchi smiled.

'Shall I forward the mail to you?'

'OK.' Ruchi's interest was waning almost as fast as it had been aroused, when Kavita said the magical words.

'There's two lakh rupees prize money for the best story.'

'Oh, yes, Kavi, send me the mail, quick, today. You are writing, na?'

'Of course.' Kavita laughed and hung up.

After delivering her thousandth untruth that she was going out to meet Kavita, Ruchi walked briskly to Inorbit Mall. Quite the pride of Vashi, she thought, as she entered. When Sanjay arrived, she was ready in her sexy avatar. When she asked to use his phone to check her mail, he let her; she would be too engrossed to stop him caressing her, and there would be more goodies later. Ruchi quickly copied the details of the mail on to the notepad on her cell phone.

Three thousand words about a story set in India, rural or urban. A story has to have a beginning, a middle, and an end, she remembered from one of the lectures she'd attended at college. A hundred ideas were swimming in her head. A love story with herself and Sanjay as the chief characters—protagonist—another word from a long-forgotten lecture, or she could write a sad story of a destitute woman. Or a vampire tale set in Vashi. *I must watch* Krrish 3 *and get some ideas from there.*

Sanjay made clumsy love to a distracted Ruchi in a dark corner of the car park, and they headed to their respective homes.

* *

Monica Kapoor, also in Mumbai, saw it a day later. She was too tired from the charity dinner she'd attended with Anil, and they both simply crashed out when they reached their lovely Cuffe Parade residence. After breakfast the next day, Anil left for work as usual; her two teenagers were at college (*We'll come home after the party, Ma*) and she was on her own, as usual. The unassuming Sushil, who had been hired to run the home smoothly, did just that. He dusted and polished and laundered and ironed and ensured that the helper lad Chotu did more of the same, that Savitribai swept and mopped every corner of the 2,500 square foot luxury apartment, that Rekha cooked everything just the way

Madam had instructed. Now all Madam had to do was kill the time on her hands.

Facebook, Candy Crush Saga, YouTube, porn (with a hasty glance over the shoulder to make sure that the servants were not entering the room). Gmail—check—the usual jokes, good, bad, pathetic ones, the sexy ones. She forwarded a few, felt a surge of excitement when she sent the dirty jokes to men. They were not close friends, just acquaintances and she did not know them very well. *Let them think what they want. Let Anil think what he wants. They are just jokes. Just sending a joke does not mean I want to sleep with them.*

She went through the whole tedious lot, expertly classifying them as 'worth a glance' and 'not worth a glance'. She sighed. She was bored, and felt vacant inside. Oh! She had almost missed one—from the Lit Club she had pretentiously joined, once upon a time. She had been a voracious reader, but when the electronic screens began invading every corner of the house, the bookshelf became a mere showpiece in Anil's study—the room where she sat now. She'd attended the Lit Club meetings for a few months, then dropped out, embarrassed that she could not find the time to read the book of the month that the members had set for themselves. The whirl of social activities unsettled her, and most of her time was taken up in organizing her wardrobe and herself, in order that she would rise to these occasions. The Lit Club began to seem too far away, or too inconvenient, or awkwardly timed.

The mail was about some short story contest. Equinox. Three thousand words, for stories by Indians, set in India. Any genre. Hmm. Worth a thought. What would Anil say? 'Why do you need to do all this? Just relax and enjoy yourself.'

Am I? Am I enjoying myself? What is that numb feeling in my head, as if I wish I was somewhere else, doing something else?

She barely concentrated on her workout at the gym. The tagline kept throwing itself back at her—*Do you have a story to tell?*

And did she want to tell her story? It was supposed to be fiction. Did she have it in her to create a tale that others would want to read? Monica had dim recollections of Nanima spinning fascinating yarns about life in Garhwal. Her mother also could hold an audience of women enthralled with her accounts of even simple recipes. Something like a Nigella Lawson—she smiled a vague apology to her mom here; her mom's gentle homely looks could not have been more different from Nigella's, but every experience that she described was as sensual as Nigella's.

The question was, was the Welham-educated Monica Kapoor, née Joshi, equal to feeling life, and then writing about it? Would other women read about it and feel inspired?

A thrill of joy! Monica realized she had made her decision.

* *

Col. (Retd.) Vikram Singh was in Mussoorie. In fact he had shifted there quite recently from Dehra Dun, which, he felt, was overpopulated with retired faujis whose only pastime was golf or cards. The family home in Doon, 36 Grant Road, was closed for the period, as he decided to spend a while in Mussoorie to follow his calling.

Vikram—with due apologies to 'Col. (Retd.)'—had seen two operations, the '62 and the '65, had been superseded and had retired in 1995 at the sprightly age of 54. He and Reema, his wife, had settled in their hometown Dehra Dun while Abhay Singh, their only son, joined the air force. He would visit them when on leave and also go trekking and holidaying with his friends. He had a sweet girlfriend and his parents loved her too. She was homely and not overly ambitious like many of the young girls of today. The family looked forward to the eventual nuptials and grandchildren. Reema had even begun shopping. And then Abhay died. Not on the battlefield defending the honour of his country, but senselessly, in a road accident on the Delhi-Dehra Dun Highway. Priyanka, his sweet little girlfriend, it turned out, was pregnant. The Singhs offered to look after her and see the child born and even raise it, but her family was consumed with shame and they moved away. The Singhs heard that Priyanka had undergone an abortion. She was now married and had moved to the mecca of anonymity—the United States of America.

Saddened and with nothing much to look forward to, Reema also died of some trivial infection and Vikram had spent the last six years on his own—sometimes golfing, sometimes playing cards, mostly wanting to get away from it all. At 73, he was not simply waiting to die, but looking forward to spending the rest of his days pleasantly and constructively. Someone mentioned Mussoorie. Vikram chose to move for a period of six months; he could always come back home if it did not suit him.

So here he was, spending six months in rented accommodation—as they say in fauji parlance. Walks in the morning, walks in the evening! On one of his walks, he met Raghav Singh. Raghav was a young man in his forties. He had been a well-to-do senior executive with Glaxo India, plodding along the corporate path, when suddenly he saw light. He sold his house, divorced his wife (their childless marriage was on the rocks, anyway) and moved lock, stock, and barrel to Mussoorie. He wrote a book—*Peace, not Paisa*—and got published, wrote again and was published again. His royalties, along with his investments, gave him a comfortable life.

You should write, Colonel. Your war stories are forgotten history—this generation needs to know them.

Many such walks and many such talks later, Vikram was really fired. Should he write a book? More importantly, he thought with wry humour, would he live to complete it? He bought a ream of paper and some pens and pencils. One day, a beaming Raghav came in; he had some news. His publishers, Indus Books Ltd, had announced a short story contest.

'It's a short story, Colonel. You can do it before you die!' he teased. 'Submission on September 22, the autumnal equinox. You can do 3,000 words. It is a good time to write. In any case, you will be cooped up inside during the rains. May as well write!'

Vikram made his decision.

'It's fiction. So cook up a good story. And there is Rs. 2,00,000 to be won, we'll cheer with Glenfiddich when you are done!' were Raghav's parting words.

* *

Maya Sinha was worried and alone. As a bright young thing in the Jesus and Mary College fifteen years ago, she had never dreamt she would be divorced and penniless. Her parents had been well-to-do, owned a flat in Defence Colony in Delhi, and gave her a good education. They would have married her off into a prosperous Punjabi family, if she had not met Rakesh Sinha, an earthy handsome hunk. She fell for the son-of-the-soil routine, married, had a son and all went reasonably well until her husband fell in love with a rich girl's money. The son-of-the-soil routine worked again, and he divorced Maya and moved, with his son, into the gullible heiress' mansion. Maya had agreed to the divorce by mutual consent because she had been too dazed to do anything else. Now she was left with just her wits, her education, no alimony, and one parent (her mother had died a few years earlier); she set about rebuilding her life.

New Delhi was overcrowded and dirty and it was no surprise when dengue sneaked in on people. But, she was not prepared for it to happen to her disciplined father in their scrupulously clean surroundings. His death by dengue left her devastated. And penniless, because the pension stopped!

She was preparing for the NET exams, which would get her a lecturer's job, hopefully a permanent one, in a reputed college. But, that would take a while. She continued to study, even as she taught English at the dingy government-unrecognized college nearby. She had just enough money to eat reasonably well. But, she had to earn more . . . save . . . best get a government job that would give her a life pension.

Someone had told her about the uncertain world of commercial writing that the Internet had spawned. There were websites and more websites, each vying with the other for customers' eyeballs. She registered on FreelanceIndia.com as she had been advised, and work had started trickling in. The work was not guaranteed, and you could be paid as low as 20 paisa per word, but it was something. In the past year, she had learnt to reject the bloodsuckers and deal only with the humans who often gave 50 paisa per word and small incentives for work well done. Her quill was nicely sharpened as she sat down that day, to dispatch her articles.

As was her wont, she scouted around for other writing jobs. She really wanted to write something other than banking articles, something more literary perhaps. Did anyone need nice essays or short stories, for instance?

Her Google search 'short stories, com' brought her to the homepage of Indus publishers—there was a short story competition. Oh well, she had meant 'short stories, commercial', but a competition was also good. In fact, a competition was better, it seemed. Rs. 2,00,000 was not a small amount and Maya was determined to win it. The page requested its visitors to 'watch this space' for forthcoming details, and so she would.

* *

Souza's was a happening place—a cosy cafe, in a rare quiet street in bustling Pune. Yet it was close enough to the living quarters of many foreign students. These were students from African nations, the Middle East, and even South-east Asia; they missed their food back home and strangely found solace in Maria Souza's Italian and Greek concoctions, not to mention the coffee and the muffins and the pies. Jerry took care of the accounts.

During the lull periods, the Souzas read. Their modest personal library was part of the shop's decor. Both enjoyed books about travel. Hugh and Colleen Gantzer, William Dalrymple, Orhan Pamuk, and Maria's favourite—*Merlyn the Magician and the Pacific Coast Highway*—were prominent on their shelves. They also enjoyed the cooking shows on TV, *Travelling Diva* being Maria's favourite. That was how she had taught herself Italian cooking. She had made no concrete plans for anything, but there was a vague sense that someday things would be better—theirs could be a specialty restaurant, they would earn more, save more, they would travel, maybe even adopt a child . . . any or all of the above.

Meanwhile, they were only too happy to serve their customers and lend a patient ear to the various problems they had studying in a foreign land—the language, the strange conservatism, the racial discrimination beneath the apparent friendliness. The most common grievance was that they were cheated of their money—whether it was a flat they wished to rent or a second-hand Kinetic Honda they wished to buy. The locals treated them with suspicion, kept their distance, and cheated them in simple matters like the purchase of vegetables or small repairs at home. The stories were legion and the Souzas often laughingly remarked that they could write a book on this whole business. The simple Goan couple gave them whatever tips they could, recommended shops where they would not be cheated, taught them how to count in Marathi (the local language), and so on.

The husband and wife duo worked very well together, the cafe ran reasonably well. But, costs were escalating each day. Yo-yo politics led to yo-yo economics, making the price of onions skyrocket one day, and the next day, sugar went through the roof. It was becoming more and more difficult to cater to their regulars without eating into their own profit margins. They were not greedy or dishonest; they did not short-change their customers, but they had to live. Maria was woefully thinking of reducing the portion size of her lasagna and moussakas. It broke their hearts.

And then—*boom*! Short circuit! It was the big transformer near the row of shops, at the end of the street. The quiet street went suddenly ablaze. The fire brigade arrived promptly, but the damage was considerable. The outer room was not too badly affected, but the kitchen and appliance section was gutted and needed complete redoing. Meanwhile, they put together two tables in the corner of the customer area. This was Maria's makeshift work area. The menu had to be curtailed to the few favourites, while the Souzas struggled with the repairs.

They were not strangers to struggle.

The municipal compensation would take a while, and even then it would not cover the entire cost. Currently the officials were busy discovering exactly what had gone wrong.

Somehow, the Souzas made the customer area habitable and carried on serving. Their regulars, the darlings, tried to come oftener, bring more friends, did their little bit to help. They came in with their laptops, worked, had that extra coffee and muffin. It was during one such act of kindness that someone stumbled upon a short story competition and Jerry and Maria learnt of Equinox.

Why not? they thought. Prize money of two lakh rupees was good. Not enough, but good. It couldn't harm. And, how long would 3,000 words take anyway? Jerry decided to write and set his brain into thinking mode.

* *

There was a hubbub in the literary world. The Economist Crossword Book Awards, 2013 were announced. This was the illustrious list—hot off the wires!

English Fiction

Twelve Tales of Summer by Sadhana Vaze

English Non-fiction

Melting Pots: Perspectives on Urban India by S. K. Gupta

Indian Language Fiction Translation

Thanjavur by A. Lakshmi

Popular Fiction

What the Dickens! by Sujoy Mitra

Children's Fiction

The Talking Tree and Other Tales by Madhavi Desai and Roshni Rai

Ramona stared at her Yahoo home page and ran her finger down the list of names again. She barely registered the others. Sadhana Vaze was where she remained transfixed.

Sadhana was a close friend of a close friend. Would she . . . would she possibly lend her name, face, voice to Equinox? It was worth a try. She could do a video for Indus. A video where she gave short story writing tips, perhaps, that had helped her in writing her prize-winning book of short stories and so on. Hmm . . . need to check with the publishers of *Twelve Tales of Summer*.

Ramona began scratching out her own dhobi list.

1 call Arnav, ask about Sadhana

2 meet Sadhana. lunch at Taj? Samovar?

3 publisher of the book

'Oh, OK, I'll find that out just now', she mumbled to herself.

She dialled a number and dictated crisply.

Within minutes her cell phone blinked a message.

She continued her list.

3 publisher of the book—New Age

Hmm . . . big, but not big enough to cause us pain. Wicked, thought Ramona.

She was confident she could swing a small promotional activity, with no legal faux pas.

4 legal guys to fine-comb

5 Face book—Tina, Hriday

She spoke on the office intercom: 'Tina, I need to see you and Hriday ASAP. Get us all on WhatsApp group, na?'

WhatsApp was quicker than the intranet.

She continued with her list.

6 sponsors—IMPORTANT

Who would want to associate with a short story prize for a period?

She drummed her fingers in consonance with the grey rain outside. Mumbai, as usual, was beautiful and ugly at the same time. The final event would be here in

September, or possibly October. It would not be raining then, she thought inconsequentially.

7 points for sponsors

- sponsor the event for at least three years
- winner award and five shortlistee awards (20,000 each)
- stay of shortlistees (2 nights, one day), Taj? Grande Palace?
- event, lunch—event managers, caterers, guest list

The phone beeped. It was the **equinox** group created by Tina. She wanted Meher Azam, her assistant and Raghu Advani of the legal department on board as well.

8888877777 Ramona

Add Meher and Raghu, Tina.

8888877777 Ramona

We meet at 1.45 pm today, after lunch, conf room 2. Meher, pls confirm

The meeting was brief and fruitful. That was classic Ramona—brief and fruitful, and in control.

'Our initial reach was by announcing on our website, mails went out to those who remain subscribed to us, and all the people who have written for us. They would probably have sent it along to interested parties. We now need a Facebook presence to drag in more people who have not yet begun to write the story. We are already running behind time here.

'Details on our website, Tina, Hriday. Snappy, small content, nice logo for FB—we need this today, is it possible?'

'The day after tomorrow.'

'We have to be more visible.'

'Sponsors—priority, Meher', continued Ramona, 'the more the merrier. Nationwide literary talent hunt, FB presence, India oriented, etc. is what they need to know . . . and anything else you can think of, Meher. Second, look at the event schedule, we'll invite the winner and the five smaller-prize winners and treat them nice, check staying arrangements, etc. Press conference—invitees, literati, catering, etc. Let's look for at least three event managers before we finalize.'

Meher scribbled furiously.

'Raghu, please draw up a contract for the Rs. 2,00,000 winner. He has to pledge his next book to us. Do we need to sugar-coat this in our statements on Facebook? Also, is Sadhana Vaze free to give us an exclusive video on short story writing tips? And, this is urgent.'

Raghu's notepad registered the two requirements.

'I am trying to meet her tomorrow, Thursday tops', Ramona continued. 'We must announce Sadhana Vaze's video with the second FB post. Let's make it happen!'

'Anything else, guys?' she thought to ask.

'This is really rushed', someone said.

'I know.' Ramona looked up from her Samsung Galaxy and smiled, a little grimly. 'We have to make a killing.'

With Equinox the competition and Equinox the anthology, Ramona Das hoped to justify her position as commissioning editor of Indus Books Ltd.

Indus was little more than a minnow. The Seths and the Dalrymples did not come to them; the big fish of the publishing sea snapped them up. They at Indus were getting by with homespun self-help books and desi chick lit. A lot of wannabes had become writers.

This was not as bad as it looked. Everyone had ideas. Everyone had 'higher education'. Many people had corporate jobs that they were sick of and needed to take a break. They wrote and Indus published on demand, kept 50 per cent of the royalty, sometimes more. These new authors did not mind at all. They were only too happy to see their name in print and to make that little buck. And, Indus kept the larger buck.

Often, these new writers were invited to colleges to lecture, simply on the basis of that one book. College campuses were also mushrooming all over the country, and they needed some literati, some illuminati. The writers made the most of these invitations, and then some maybe went back to their corporate jobs. Or they wrote another book if a partner could keep the home fires burning during that period. No one starved, everyone was happy—the publisher, the writer, the reader.

So many people were writing; even India's exploding population could not produce enough readers for those many writers. Reading habits were changing. These days it did not matter if you had not read a particular author. Writers could, at best, hope for a niche following. Fifty years ago, a well-read person would be embarrassed at not having read Dickens or Henry James. In the professional field of teaching literature or of writing, you had to have read Shakespeare and maybe even Chaucer, and at least attempted the Iliad and the Odyssey in the original. And poetry! It was not enough to know the Romantic poets or the difference in the prosody of an ode and an elegy—you had to be able to quote from the great masters.

But, writing (and reading) was truly democratized these days. There were fewer takers each year for the study of English literature. Young people were unashamedly Indian but had not necessarily troubled to read classical Indian authors. Many preferred easy reads. Others were Rowling or Tolkien fans! And sci-fi had its tribe of faithful followers. Young adults wore this particular brand of literacy on their sleeves. And their memories and attention spans simply did not allow for quoting. Instead, they would whip the fanciest mobile out of their pockets and Google a quote, an author name, or the name of a book or the entire book, if it was free.

Or perhaps, that was just too harsh. They, young adults, just read a lot of books that their parents and teachers had simply not been exposed to. Fantasy fiction, the new creature called young adult fiction, chick lit, and the latest craze, mythological fiction, speculative fiction—books today defied the boundaries of genre and style. Anything and everything was a book.

Poetry had gone the same way. Free verse had made itself popular several decades ago. Ezekiel, Kolatkar, Gieve Patel—these guys were studied on college campuses in India. They perhaps paved the way for newer generations of free-verse writers. The lyrical beauty of Kalidasa's verse or of Wordsworth, or the textured poesy of Yeats or Eliot had given way to the more prosaic and the less allusive. You just broke the sentence—strategically—to form an uneven verse, with a jagged edge, and that was poetry. Some liked it and some didn't. It did not matter. There was no gold standard in writing. Whatever worked for the reader was good.

And so people wrote—good, bad, and mediocre books were published and small publishers had to rise to meet this new challenge. They had to come up with translations or innovative anthologies.

Equinox was the offspring of this challenge and Ramona's fertile brain. An anthology of short stories by Indian writers, about India—it was just the shot in the arm Indus needed. Novels took too long. The competition and the anthology would be called Equinox; the prefix *equi* was the focus. Equinox literally meant equal night (and thus implied equal day) and this was the sunnier meaning Ramona was reinforcing. Equal night and equal day, equal opportunity for all, an opportunity for writers and non-writers to balance or equalize the positives and negatives in their lives, rise to the occasion and produce something worthwhile. Whatever it was, Equinox sounded good—intriguing. And then having the submissions come in on the autumnal equinox! It was a publicity gimmick. Well, why not? It made the name meaningful and lent respectability to Indus' nebulous image. They cared about knowledge and facts and erudition, the title seemed to suggest. The team had arrived at it after rejecting several predictable titles like Lekhak and IndiaWrites and far-fetched ones like Topaz and Vinculum, which meant a connecting medium—but no one would get it. There was a Rose Day and a Hug Day and a Whatchamacallit Day. Indus would mint an Equinox Day.

The next step was to give this event far and wide publicity, connect with writers and potential writers through probably the social media; announce small, but attractive gifts in addition to the Rs. 2,00,000. Also the promise of good publicity after the victory, perhaps even commissioning them for another story—it would help both the writer and Indus.

* *

priest and nun scandal

Manorama Yearbook—events of a year in the life of a girl called Manorama . . .

Nah . . . sounds dumb

aging actress or poet based on Kamala Das

story of a spa

These were the entries 'scratched' into Rambler's electronic notepad. He could not believe it was taking him this long to even arrive at the subject of his short story. He had once seen a way-out film called *Sona Spa*, and parts of it had stuck. Need he write only about Kerala?

Well, he was not going to be travelling for a while, maybe a month. It made sense to write what he saw. He wondered if he had overreached. He was so used to trotting the globe, throwing his random thoughts together and producing the travel writing that his editors loved, that this writer's block was a novel experience. His jaw set beneath the curly beard and he decided he simply had to do it. He *was* a writer, for Pete's sake.

The subject! The subject!

Rambler took to walking around the fields on the muddy foot tracks, for inspiration. The farmhands were amused and indulgent towards this madman with his fancy gadgets, not doing any work. City folk could seldom soil their hands, they thought. Chettan was not pleased.

Chettan was Rambler's elder brother, Sunny Kutty. He had more troubles on his farm than he had farmhands. Each one of them needed to pull their weight. The rice harvest time was nearing, and the crops had to be guarded. Once the harvest was gathered, roughly in early August, then was the time for relaxation and merry-making; that was the famous Onam festival with the legendary boat races. Until then, people worked really hard.

When Chettan admonished Rambler with these arguments, it only fired his imagination. Should he participate in the boat race and then write about it? He had covered it in a magazine earlier in his career.

Um, it's far too predictable—when in Kerala, write about the boat race. He rubbished the idea.

Or, maybe he could write about the people who sponsored these races. There was bound to be a political-commercial connect. Hmm . . . There was a lot of finding out to do. Politics in Kerala was a ticking bomb. He was amazed at what he did not know. For instance, he was not sure how much of the Kerala coastline had been affected by the 2004 tsunami; were people resettled, this late in 2013? Or did they still bear the scar?

He Googled 'Kerala'—the Onam festival, the rice harvest, political parties and chief ministers, past and present . . . phew . . . this could take forever. The wider he searched, the deeper he felt he needed to dig. How about weaving an intriguing plot about one of the coastal towns affected by the tsunami? He checked out the names of towns. So many of them had changed— Quilon was now Kollam, Trichur was Thrissur, Cochin was Kochi, and of course, Allepey had become Alapuzha—all shed and shorn of the anglicization. These earlier names were easier on the Indian tongue, he supposed—somehow it felt like the cities had changed their character as well. He hadn't been there in years, felt nothing for them. Maybe he'd flown over them on his way to Sri Lanka. What could he do about them? Write about a scene on a railway station that he remembered from childhood? Well, that would be generic—happening anywhere.

Did he want to write a human interest story? Or, something funny? Like Tenali Raman of Madurai? He would have to do a lot of manufacturing, conjure up a fictitious king (else mine extensively through the history of Kerala) and his jester and then think up situations that were plausible in that era. He was warming to the idea of funny. Things were far too unfunny at present. What could be funny? His interactions with his elder brother? The widowed schoolteacher who made eyes at Chettan irrespective of his marital status? Jagadeesan's lazy son? (Jagadeesan was a senior worker on their plantation). Or the number of people who migrated as nurses and ayahs and any other kind of professionals? There was still a mad scramble to get to Mesket, the Malayali pronunciation of Muscat.

Better look around and write about what he saw. It was July already. Maybe he would just start writing and see where it went.

He stared at the computer screen; it stared back at his vacant mind. If he had a pencil, he would be chewing its end right now. He was back at his favourite tea shop, with the cup of tea cooling before him. Ganesan sat behind his table and its glass jars of biscuits, pondering over some accounts. Groups of men came and went. Never a group of women or even young girls, Rambler noted absently. Maybe they went to the better restaurants and cafes.

Rambler swatted away at flies, watched some more customers finish their tea and dissolve into the rain. He had forgotten his umbrella again. He prayed for a sunny day and for an inspiring idea.

* *

The young girl wanted to do something constructive with her life. She did not want to do what her parents wished, i.e., get married and be a wife and mother. She was a Mumbai girl and Mumbai girls were smart.

Ruchi surveyed her first literary creation and felt dissatisfied. It was not interesting. And, it was clear she was writing about herself. Why could she not write like the lovely classical novels that she had never bothered to read? Everyone else liked them.

I don't have to write a novel. It's a short story. I must read a few short stories before I write mine. They did not have a computer at home; they were getting one this Diwali. Should she go to a cybercafé? It was still raining. Sanjay? No, she was just not in the mood.

Kavita had suggested O. Henry and Oscar Wilde. 'Why so quiet, Ruchi?' her mother questioned her about her uncharacteristic thoughtful mood. Ruchi told her about the competition. Mrs. Sharma expressed disbelief at the prize money. '*Buddhu banaa rahe hain*'—she was clear that 'they' were making fools out of gullible, ordinary folks. Whoever heard of people in these one-room dwellings coming up with literary gems? Theirs was the onus to live the *grahasth jeevan*—live like worldly-wise householders. All this dreaming and writing stories and verse was for someone else. She, however, did mention Munshi Premchand as the epitome in Hindi fiction. '*Zara pyaaz kaat de, beta.*' She asked Ruchi to chop some onions.

Ruchi turned on the TV for inspiration. Maybe she could write the story of a movie and no one would know. As she chopped an onion for her mother's curry, she thought of *Listen Amaya*, a really offbeat film that Kavi had dragged her to. The theatre had been empty then, not many people can have watched it. *Hmm . . . I'll try that, I can always change the story a little.*

She flipped channels with her onion-smelly hand. DD Bharati. The newspaper had listed a teleplay based on Premchand's story Gaban. It was set in a village and was about poor farmers and their daughter's dowry or something. It was nice, but seemed too long. This was the fourth episode.

And I will have to watch it every time until the story ends.

OK, I will try to write the story of Listen Amaya. *I will call it something else.*

After lunch, Ruchi settled down with a few loose papers, near the window overlooking the fountain. How she wished that computer would arrive before that damned autumnal equinox and not later, at Diwali. Oh, well, she would type it out later at the cybercafé.

Deepti, a widow, ran a cafe and a library in a beautiful area of the lovely city of Bangalore. She called it Book a Coffee. Her daughter Amaya helped her when she had the time. Many young and old people came and helped in the cafe. They also sat and had coffee and paid for it. The students were nice and friendly and one of them liked Amaya. An older man, Farouque, also came regularly and sat with his laptop. Deepti wondered what he did for a living, he seemed to spend so much time there. But he was nice, and Deepti also started liking him. They became friends and then lovers.

One day, Amaya found them together—they were not really sleeping together, but maybe they had, because the sheets were rumpled. Amaya was upset and refused to talk to her mother. She told Deepti that she would leave the house if she married Farouque. Naturally, Deepti told Farouque not to come; after all, children are more important.

They did not meet for a while. Amaya noticed that her mother was very sad. She went and said, 'Mummy, it is OK. You want to marry Farouque Uncle. I will be all right.' Deepti asked her if she was sure. When Amaya assured her that she would not mind, Deepti and Farouque decided to get married.

Two hundred and twenty-six words only. How on earth was she to write 3,000? The story was already over. And she had used the actors' off-screen names—Deepti and Farouque. *What else to add*?

'It is plagiarism, idiot', Kavita told her over the phone, after she had finished reading it out. 'Make your own story. And add dialogues, describe the places . . . I told you about O. Henry.'

'I don't have any of his books, and where do I go looking for them now? Books cost so much.'

'Do you remember "The Gift of the Magi", we had it in our school textbook? Write a story like that—it's a complete story, like a full circle.'

'Oh, I know, I will sit in the Crossword at Inorbit and read there. They let you read there. Message me a few author names, Kavi. I will go there now.'

'No Sanjay?'

'He's busy . . . shh . . . chal, bye, Kavita', she spoke her friend's name loudly, deliberately to reassure her mother who had lowered the volume of the TV and was pretending not to listen to Ruchi's conversation.

* *

SUMMER ROMANCE
Gulmohur Palace
12th August 1968

Dear Prince R,

It was a delight meeting you at the luncheon today.

I do look forward to your august company at the Gymkhana Summer Ball on the 15th of August.

Yours faithfully,

Arunima Devi

* *

Udai Bhawan
13th August 1968

Dear Princess Arunima,

You do me a great honour. Indeed, it is a truth that Udaipur is that much brighter for the presence of yourself and your two younger sisters, this season.

Please do me the honour of at least one dance at the ball.

Yours faithfully,

Raghubir

* *

Gulmohur Palace
16th August 1968

Dear Prince R,

You praise me to the skies and then take your own
time asking me to dance. What shall I make of this?
And who was that ravishing creature in the red sari
that you danced with twice?

Yours faithfully (and a little miffed),

Arunima Devi

    * *

Udai Bhawan
16th August 1968

My dear princess,

Please do not be miffed (how charmingly you put it) at me, for then surely I will have to break all convention and visit you at the Gulmohur Palace, and what would your esteemed father, Raja Bir Singh, make of that? You do, I am sure, understand that as a friend of the host, I have to dance the obligatory dances. And you, my dear, did not seem lacking in partners either! The clean-shaven gentleman, for instance, whom you gave three dances?

Yours ever,

Raghubir

* *

Udai Bhawan
18th August 1968

My dear Princess Arunima,

May I assume that our little misunderstanding is cleared? I hope to see you at the governor's dinner tomorrow.

Yours,

Raghubir

* *

Gulmohur Palace
18th August 1968

Dear Prince R,

I do apologize for not responding to your earlier missive. I was a little indisposed.

I have been thinking about what you said, what my dear father would think if you were to call for me. Dear Pitaji is an indulgent father, especially since Mataji's demise three years ago. He would probably encourage you to court me.

I would be at the governor's dinner tomorrow, if I feel well enough.

Yours ever,

Arunima Devi

    * *

Gulmohur Palace
20th August 1968

My dear Prince R,

I am sorry to have missed the governor's dinner. But I do wonder if you missed me at all, since I received no communication from you to that effect.

Have I been too forward in mentioning that my dear father might encourage you to court me? It is not incumbent upon you to do so, although I would not resist if you did. Perhaps . . .

Yours ever,

Arunima Devi

* *

Maybe this missive is a little forward, but then I am known as an unconventional maiden. Even as I write 'maiden', I smile to myself, because my feelings for you are far from being modest and maidenly.

Monica was not sure where she would fit this in, but it sounded nice.

She counted. Four hundred and sixty-eight words. Long way to go, thought Monica. She loved romances and she wanted to make this quite the epic piece. Her head was brimming with ideas. Himachali royalty, Rajasthani royalty, Scarlett O'Hara, Shyam Benegal's *Zubeidaa*, the intricate narratives in M. M. Kaye's *The Far Pavilions*— these were all trying to escape and find expression. These stories, novels, and movies held an enduring appeal for Monica. *Do people remember the short stories they read? I do remember Chekhov, Lawrence.* She did not presume to place herself in the same category as these masters, but she could create a vibrant piece of work. Much as she admired Chekhov's short stories (she had not been there in a while, but school and college lessons had gotten into the habit of coming back to her these days), it was the heroic, romantic sagas that had pride of place in her heart.

Horses and elephants and polo and waltzes would definitely be part of her tale; to her, they were the grand, eternal motifs of romance. She had done her bit of Googling (thank God for these guys!) and thinking. Her story would be set in the period just prior to the dissolution of the privy purses—*I must describe the dresses well.* Since it was to be a short summer romance, it would begin in August and end with the polo season. She would retain the mystery of why Raghubir did not quickly and openly propose to the comely Arunima; that would come out in the end. *God, I love this language. Comely was such a lovely word,* she thought. Meanwhile, the letters were to get longer and more passionate, while maintaining the grace of royalty. *I think I will add one very passionate meeting alone; they will kiss, a lot, but not do anything a lot more than that.*

A story written through letters implied a very deep understanding and love between the two people involved. You did not meet so often, but the written word conveyed the full flavour of the emotion. At least in her world, it did.

Monica's voice of reason also made itself heard. She'd had a somewhat bumpy ride and she had learnt life's lessons. Romance and love were pretty tales that people told themselves. Nevertheless, falling in love, even briefly, was one of the most glorious human experiences and that was good enough reason to write about them.

Her story would be aesthetic and heart-warming and to hell with cynics.

* *

Vikram was excited. His mind did stray back occasionally to his comfortable study in Dehra Dun, and to his military history notes lying in the right-hand-side top drawer. But he had paid six months' rent for this place in Mussoorie and it would not be refunded. He just made the best of what there was. His pension demanded this bit of financial prudence.

This little flat was not too bad. True, it did not have that fantastic view of the valley and the far-off mountains. It, in fact, was crowding into the rock face and the sun did not stream in joyously each day. However, it had a certain seclusion and charm, in spite of the dampness. And since it was raining most of the time, the sun did not matter. No one got the sun. The side of the mountain that he faced was lush and green, and post-rains, there would be a profusion of wildflowers.

It was also quieter, because it was on the 'backside', the estate agent had said; he had to come out and down, and then walk around the building to reach the main road. No one could see him until he did that. He was not alarmed that he was not immediately visible from the road. There was a landline (cell phones sometimes did not work). Also the plumbing was functional and efficient, and that mattered more than panoramic views.

He had called in a boy everyday to cook and clean for him. By cook, he meant that the boy delivered hot food cooked by his mother, at an appointed time each day. He washed the used dishes immediately. He made good, strong, sweet tea, gave him a steaming cup and stored the rest in a thermos flask for Vikram to have until it was formally teatime in the afternoon. He made sure there was an adequate supply of Marie digestive biscuits, which he bought at the tiny store downstairs—acidity was Vikram's one big fear.

The boy, Bhado, also dusted and cleaned and tidied his bed and polished his shoes with an enthusiasm that would put the most loyal of military orderlies to shame. Today, he sensed the old dadaji's excitement—he had come in earlier than usual (that was to be his new timing) with two hot parathas and sabji. While Dadaji had it on the makeshift dining table, he swept vigorously and lovingly dusted the writing table at the window. Mussoorie loved writers. Ruskin Bond had prepared it for literary fame!

'*Wahan ki cheezein hatao mat*' came the old man's directive to leave the study table paraphernalia alone. Breakfast done, Vikram organized his pen, pencils, and notepad in writing position, and arranged the sheaf of crisp white blank paper squarely at the far end of the table. He was dressed for the occasion in T-shirt and trousers, socks and slippers, hair recently clipped and neatly brushed.

'65 operations

- *1948-POK was formed, part of Poonch district already in Pakistan*

- *1964, June, infiltrators on Mendhar sector*

- *steady attack, Pak did not back off in the winter, as is normally done*

- *massive tank battles in the plains of Punjab*

- *Poona Horse, Tarapore lost his life, India lost Tarapore*

- *Pak lost many more men than India and eventually surrendered*

- *travelling up and down in convoys for food supply to Leh, more than 200 three tons to stock up for the winter*

- *travails of the EME workshop-detachment at Leh, . . . , an open field near Udhampur*

-   *they had had to repair practically overnight
    all the vehicle casualties*

I remember the young EME major who spoke of his young pregnant wife, whom he had hastily dispatched to Pathankote, and left her to make her way to her parents in Maharashtra for the delivery. The young man had also spoken of his father dying at the same time, how he had rushed there and then rushed right back.

Vikram had been stationed at Leh during the 1965 operations. He had not been married then, so had had fewer worries than the young major, Deshpande, whom he had met. He had also not been worried about his parents, as his elder brother was with them. Amongst Garhwalis, it was tradition to send sons into the army. They had seen many war casualties and were therefore more accepting of them, even as they coped with the loss of a loved one.

As he was doing now, at the age of 75—no parents, no wife, no son, no brother, sister-in-law in far-off Vishakhapatnam with her naval officer son. Vikram viewed his situation dispassionately and made more notes—*need to—see maps to refresh memory, get exact dates of infiltration in Mendhar sector, exact number of war casualties, names of all the war heroes.*

Vikram viewed his notes several times and just did not know where to begin. His A4 sheets remained pristine and his pencils sat at the precise angle at which he had laid them down. And he, with his hands on the table—elbows off, of course—pondered. Nothing!

* *

Maya woke up with a jumbled head. Not an aching head, but a jumbled one. Well, first things first. She made herself a cup of tea and dunked her Glucose biscuits in it—a habit she had picked after her marriage. It was a Sunday, and she needed to study for the NET. But that wretched Rajinder's Junior College and Academy had lined up two extra classes for her today, 2 p.m. to 4 p.m. There went the afternoon nap, or to be more precise, there went the afternoon half-hour when she lay on bed trying to sleep but ended up worrying about money instead.

She let the maid in to sweep and mop. The laundry she did herself. Her mother's semi-automatic machine worked just fine. She cooked and cleaned and washed up herself, too. It was just her and she hardly ever cooked elaborate meals for herself. And then Delhi had any number of cheap takeaways.

She bathed and prepared a sketchy meal of chaawal-daal; she doffed her hat to fresh greens by adding some spinach in the dal. That done, she settled down to correct the papers of the previous assignment. She must finish these and carry them back with her at two. When she came back, she would do her commercial writing assignments, and then she wanted to watch *Kabhi Khushi Kabhi Gham* on TV. She had seen it a zillion times, but today she was just in the mood for a rerun, a nice comfortable rerun, with the unfailing entertainer Shahrukh Khan—it would make her feel she was with an old and loving friend.

The story! What should I write about? Her mind grappled with this dilemma as she kept marking her papers with the ease of long practice. Well, she could write about the substandard education Rajinder's Junior College dished out. *But I need my job. I can't expose them.*

In her mind's eye, she went over her students— Kamaldeep the stationery shop owner's daughter, Sandeep Mehta the I-know-I-am-a-stud (the girls swooned over him, and he was not above giving even her, his teacher, the glad eye). He would make a good subject. His journey from vacant student to leering adult might be an interesting read. What about Reena Malik, her colleague, who dressed far too provocatively for a college teacher?

What about Nirbhaya? That horrifying rape that had shaken the nation? Her mind parked itself there, as her hands completed the task at hand.

Maya went through her extra classes mechanically, not that she was an insincere teacher. She simply was not motivated enough. Her students went through the motions of learning. They were far more interested in their mobiles, their friends, and their Facebook friends. And she did not think it was part of her duties to get them interested in the learning process. *Their primary school teachers should have done that*, she often grumbled to herself. They were now supposed to want to learn more; they were supposed to be eager to make careers and to want to contribute to society. That probably happened in an ideal world, but not in Rajinder's Junior College. The students, the staff, the administrative staff, the trustees—all played out their parts in the charade that was education and then went home to their TVs, computers, iPads, mobile phones, and families.

Nirbhaya occupied her mind as she walked back in the 5 p.m. heat. The official monsoon had hit the western coast, but Delhi was in dryness. As it would be for most of the year! The fabulously constructed roads that she measured with her brisk pace would do the nation's capital proud, if only they were not littered with garbage bins and the homes of pavement dwellers.

She slowed down and looked around. There were stories happening everywhere. A girl, not more than ten, dry dark skin, lustreless brown hair was transporting goods on a cycle cart, her little sister (brother?) braving it along with the cartons at the back. Where were the parents? Had they put them up to this? Or were the children destitute? Working by day and hiding from sexual predators at night?

And do I really want to write about these depressing realities?

Sex does sell, but do I have any right to sell it when I do precious little to stop and help anyone?

The golgappa vendor, possibly a Bangladeshi refugee (India was full of them now) might make a good story— if only he would tell the truth. The half-blind woman selling useless little brooms and *chataai* fans? Where did she come from? Where did she source her things? How much did she earn? Where did she live? What did she eat? Did she have children? And did she conceive them on the footpath? Did the father of her children stay with her or had he run away to a more attractive woman?

And, most importantly, will she tell me all these things if I ask? And, do I dare to ask at all?

Maya reached home and went about her tasks. By 9 p.m., she was comfortably ensconced in her favourite chair in front of the TV. A notebook and pencil were testimony to her decision to jot down ideas for the competition story.

When the film ended, Maya went off to bed. Her notepad bore three words—*research for Nirbhaya*.

* *

Since the fire, Maria had been waking up in the middle of the night, perspiring through a nightmare. 'Why?' she had asked herself crossly. The fire had damaged the shop, but not destroyed it. They had a roof over their heads—the pleasing rented flat where they lived. The landlady was friendly and only too glad to have law-abiding citizens who paid the rent in time, so it was not like they would be evicted and become homeless.

Jerry too was disturbed, though he coped more successfully than Maria. He did not have nightmares but he could not stop thinking about it; that haunting fear returned again and again. The fear of homelessness, of joblessness, went back to their days in Goa.

Maria and Jerry used to run Souza Cottage, a homestay facility in the Colva village of South Goa. The beach was never as crowded as the more popular ones of North Goa, and that ensured a trickle of peace-loving visitors almost all through the year. They did try to close down for three months in a year during the rains, but did not always succeed. Good-naturedly, they worked their annual repairs and maintenance even as they entertained their sporadic monsoon visitors. They thanked God for his grace and enjoyed their work time as much as they would a holiday.

One fine day, Natasha landed up. She was a pretty 25-year-old Russian girl who needed the peace to write a book. Her disciplined habits were easy on the Souzas and they delighted in her presence. They had lovely chatty dinners each night, when Natasha was free after her day's work. Natasha would help Maria clear up and they would chat some more over brandy, watching the pelting rain through the lace curtains.

'Mama has to look after Father,' Natasha volunteered as she fondly thought of her dearest Mamochka tending to her father after his heart attack. She also had a brother Alexis. No boyfriend. 'Later, after I write *my Anna Karenina*,' she had said smilingly.

October brought a planeload of Russian tourists. Natasha had made friends with some of them. They all stayed at the more expensive resorts, but Natasha continued with the Souzas. She, however, would stay out the whole day and return at night, not wanting her dinner. Maria and Jerry missed her, but shrugged and carried on, they had to; she would leave them when she was done, she would have to.

One fine November morning, the 17th, Natasha did not come down for breakfast. Concerned that she was ill, Maria took up a hearty breakfast on a tray. She knocked and entered—and reeled in shock. Natasha was lying in bed—buck naked and *dead*. The room was a mess, as if it had been searched. *I wonder why?* Maria had thought dazedly. *What valuables did she possess? Did she have a lot of money?* And then, overcome with anguish: *We slept through all this? While someone was murdering that sweet girl, we were fast asleep?*

The police came and asked a lot of questions. Jerry told them about the party of Russian tourists up at the resort. They had vanished overnight. Why had it happened? Drugs, money, or something else? No one knew. Maria could barely enter the room. They packed all her belongings and kept it in the garage; it hardly made sense to send her belongings to Russia. Was the address real anyway? And had Natasha been who she said she was? The police eventually closed the case, but the neighbours would not. Stories of ghosts and haunted rooms were abuzz in the market place. It was all very unsettling.

The Souzas had fewer and fewer guests that season. And then . . . no more guests. Sadly, they sold off their home at a ridiculous price and moved to Pune to start a new life. They were just beginning to lose that feeling of despair, of limbo. And now the short circuit! It had closed the circle and brought them where they were, on the brink of uncertainty.

Maria and Jerry talked. They realized that they were unsettled; they needed to know what had happened with the Natasha case. It was haunting them. 'Could we have done something more for Natasha, Jerry?' Maria voiced the concern that they had conveniently run away from an unpleasant situation. They could not suppress their fears anymore and realized that they should bring it up and out and away. They also had to have the faith that they would not have bad luck only. There was always good interspersed with bad; that was life and the Lord would look out for them.

Meanwhile, they had to help themselves, get it out of their systems. A writing cure was a good thing, at least better than visiting a psychiatrist or a past-life regressionist that their landlady recommended 'in order to get the kinks out of one's head'.

'Let's both write Natasha's story, and then send the better one for that Equinox competition', suggested Maria.

* *

15th August—Happy Independence Day from Indus!

HELLO! All of you out there, keep that writing arm strong!

Indus expects an Exhilarating Equinox.

If you are on board, writing or encouraging or simply watching, Follow Indus, Like Indus, and Friend Indus!

There's Rs. 2,00,000 to be won!

And five prizes of Rs. 20,000!

You can do it!

Ramona liked the logo and passed the text.

* *

8888877777 Ramona

Get the ball rolling for now, guys, but we can do better.

8888877777 Ramona

Meeting Sadhana Vaze today. She can do vid, she said, with some conditions—we have to mention New Age as her publishers. Well, they are, so it's fine. We are interested in her short stories. I guess we scratch their back this one time.

8888877777 Ramona

Need script for that video, then we record and upload it. Meher, need small film-maker, recording studio. Keep them standing by while I work out how exactly to do it with Sadhana. Google her details and get them to prepare a rough script, OK?

8888877764 Meher

Ramona, going with Filmwala. They were good last time. Keep you posted.

8888877777 Ramona

K, Meher. Am leaving to meet Sadhana in a while.

* *

'Hi, Sadhana. Ramona Das. Thanks for meeting up with me at such short notice.'

'My pleasure. So tell me—'

'A coffee and something . . . ?'

They were at Samovar, the delectable cafe at the Jehangir Art Gallery.

'Just coffee, thanks.'

Ramona ordered cappuccino and kebab rolls. 'Do try them, they are delicious.'

'Sadhana, Indus has launched a short story competition, and we want it to be an interactive process with the participants. We have a Facebook page, and we wondered if you would do a video for us, with short story tips and all, you know . . . so the participants can get a boost every now and then. There will be other things as well, but only one video—yours.'

'Hmm . . . Oh . . . kay, why not? When do you want to do this? I have to go to Delhi next week, so after that? I could ask my agent—'

'Sadhana, Sadhana, I really need this favour. Arnav was very positive about *your* positive response.' Ramona was persuasive.

'Please consider it for him. And, could it be before your Delhi trip? We are really in a race against time, here. Crazy deadline. If you can spare two days, I think, we should be able to get a ten minute script ready, and shoot it tomorrow. I'll check with Filmwala. I don't think we will need anything much. You against a captivating background, and maybe a copy of *Twelve Tales*.'

'Give me a minute, I will check with Meher.'

Sadhana munched her kebab, sipped her coffee, and consulted her phone diary.

'Meher . . . yeah, yeah, I called. What's the scene with Filmwala? When can he be with us? Hmm . . . hmm . . . no, I was waiting for the details before I finalise it with her. Hmm . . . OK, bye.'

'Yes, Sadhana, please, give us an immediate slot. See if you can spare tomorrow and the day after, and we will wind it up.'

'I will give it a thought, Ramona. I'll let you know by the evening, shall I?'

'Sure. We are looking at Rs. 50,000, all told, for this little project. We would hold all rights to the film. You would also have to be present at the final event. We do deduct tax at source, by the way. I'll wait for your call, OK?'

Sadhana confirmed within two hours. Ramona had known she would, Indus had really stretched itself with that fifty thousand for Sadhana. She dialled a number— she had to work on the sponsor and/or partner for the event.

Sadhana was to report at the Indus office at 9 a.m. the next day, sign on the dotted line, and begin work. Indus would arrange for her safe transport, and meals, of course, also hand-hold, cajole, soothe, and flatter her until the end of the event.

It was arranged that Jay Kapoor of Filmwala would work on the script with Sadhana the next day; they would finalize the pre-production business, costumes, venue, etc. And the day after that, Sunday, they would shoot in the Indus conference room, and partly in Filmwala's tiny studio.

16th August

8888877777 Ramona

Raghu, pls start work on contract for winner—he gets Rs 2,00,000, he has to give us, exclus, his next book or next three short stories.'

Meher, look after Sadhana. Infrm accts 50K for her.

8888877764 Meher

Accts will need invoice frm her, will tk care

Managing shoot, booking for 6 at Grande Palace 15th Oct, also conf room for event

8888877777 Ramona

Bummer, actually. Wud have liked event on Sept 22. Too late now. Oh, wait ... suppose we say on FB, to submit by 31st Aug, so event can be on Sept 22nd?

8888877532 Tina

RAMONA!

8888877777 Ramona

Yeah, OK, OK, 15th Oct is fine for the event. Mention this in FB updates, pls, Tina

8888877764 Meher

Give the event to Emphasis or BizWhiz?

8888877777 Ramona

Bizwhiz, Meher. Formal, but fun, and not stiff

8888877543 Raghu

Stiff? LOL ☺ Meher—it's going to be in public, you know!

8888877777 Ramona

Raghu:)

8888877543 Raghu

:)

8888877532 Tina

Ramona, chk mail for new FB updates

* *

Ramona's cubicle was a sight; Post-its decorated her work station, both her phones blinked an incessant stream of messages. It reflected the current state of her organized mind; it was receiving and filing 24/7. She had to make this work for Indus. Her standing depended on it. She was quite calm actually, but really very busy. It was an organized mess, if that was possible, and Ramona was completely at home in it.

She now called a conference of all editors.

* *

8888877777 Ramona

Meher, water, coffee, biscuits in the conf room 1 by 6 pm, please

* *

They had to work out the editorial team for the Equinox entries.

Ram Mohan the chief and four others—Vidya, Melvin, Geeta, and Usha.

'What about that children's project, sir?' Vidya inquired of Ram Mohan. 'That was important—'

'Yes, but not urgent. Let's all of you work on this. Put all your eggs in one basket and watch that basket! He he!'

'Once this is over—October 15?' He continued as Ramona nodded. 'You get back to whatever you were doing, and Ramona manages this. In any case, you do have time to work on the children's project until the entries actually start coming in. Yes, Melvin.'

'Good to have something to do. Not a good deal of poetry coming in these days.' Ram Mohan grunted at Melvin's tactless truth, while the others smiled.

'We are stating categorically that midnight of September 22 is the last moment for submissions, nothing will be accepted after that. We have no idea how many entries we will have. There could be hundreds or thousands—'

'Or very few', Vidya interjected, blackly.

'Tina, can the website stop accepting submissions after midnight of September 22?'

'Let's just ignore the ones that come in after.' Tina's hand chop emphasized the logic of her statement.

'Our FB page has gone live, look it up, people. I'll keep sending you an update, Ram . . . send an update to all of you', Ramona concluded.

Despite themselves, the team felt the stirrings of interest.

* *

Rambler did get one weakly sunny day, interspersed with showers. He simply walked around the town, deliberately choosing the quieter lanes. He was used to this; it was part of his profession as travel writer, to meander along strange lanes in strange cities of unknown lands. His stocky Syrian-Christian looks could be mistaken for Goan or Greek or anyone Oriental, which meant he could walk around in many places without arousing too much attention. And he always liked to dress like the locals. Now, he was in a lungi (although many of the locals had now taken to Bermuda shorts) and shirt.

His walk took him to a few paddy fields, chock-a-block with residences, sandwiched between coir factories, or should he call them workshops for the modest spaces they occupied? Young and old women, young and old men, worked hard at converting the coconut husk into more Welcome mats similar to those stacked outside a shack. His keen eye took in the checked saris of the old women, the entire sari tucked all round the waist with no *pallu* to cover the bosom and then fall over the shoulder. The sultry climate dispensed with the need for this cumbersome modesty. The younger women were in cotton gowns or maxis while the men were in half-lungis and nothing else. They were all busy and sweating and Rambler wondered if they would make anything other than the mats, pretty though they were.

Well, God has certainly made something prettier, he thought, as he spotted a young woman emerge from one of the huts. 'I will come tomorrow', she called out in Malayalam and walked away briskly.

As he walked on, eyes roving and seeking out a story idea, he mulled over the research he had done earlier. 'I know so little about Kerala, even Allepey—Alapuzha', he corrected himself, a little ashamed, as he recalled the Wikipedia map. The blue shape had showed Alapuzha as one of the two most densely populated districts in Kerala, with fishery, coir, and tourism being its chief industries (well, that he sort of knew). The article had showered the Alapuzha backwaters with fulsome praise, and the pictures were divine. He thought it was interesting that Alapuzha was a geographical name given to the land, describing its position between the sea and network of rivers flowing into it. There were six rivers in this Venice of the East. He had Googled more pictures, cursed his stupidity, and then decided to just step out and walk about the real place. And so here he was, loosed from the confines of his blue screen, breathing in the flavour of his homeland.

He took a motorbike the next day, toured the backwaters. They were dotted with lifeboats, even though it was 'the wrong season to be in Kerala'. Tourist discounts were heavy and many places remained open. Clearly, God's Own Country had stiff competition from other popular tourist destinations of India. It was so beautiful. A snatch of a hymn came unbidden to his mind—'Through clouds and sunshine, abide with me.' Was he calling God? He could not remember the last time that he had done that. I mean, he did go to church off and on, but he forgot about it almost as soon as he came out. Maybe he would go this Sunday with Chettan and Chethathi Amma, his sister-in-law.

On a whim, he parked his bike and asked for a boat ride. It had started raining again, and the boatswain (Rambler remembered that quaint Middle-English term from his school poetry) looked at him like he had taken leave of his senses. 'Wait', he said. Rambler was quite content to sit around in the closest shack and sip more tea. He thought of the pretty girl near the coir workers' huts. She had said she would be there today as well. Would she be there tomorrow? He would take a gander there tomorrow again. *Oh, it's Sunday! Well, after church then.*

He fell into a conversation with Friedrich, a German tourist on a 'spiritual' holiday. He had been friends with the Indian professor who taught Sanskrit at Tubingen University, where he taught Comparative Religion. He had learnt a lot about India from her. He had given up his job to come here. He woke at 4 a.m., learnt yoga as per the schedule set by his guru-trainer. He followed a strict Ayurvedic cure regime, customized for him. 'I eat vegetarian food, sometimes fish.'

'Do I miss the German wurst and black pudding? No, I have it there when I go back. Too hot here', he claimed. He could live here forever, he declared, if he got a work permit. He would train at the spa, if he could extend his tourist visa.

'Kerala is different from the rest of India. I loved Benares', he pronounced in his peculiar German way, 'but it gets noisy. And there is not so much water and green. And the River Ganges . . . so sad now!'

'Have you seen the rest of Kerala?'

'A little bit. Alapuzha . . . it is different.'

Rambler almost asked the question most Indians are accused of asking—whether he was married or divorced or what. He decided it did not matter. Friedrich moved on because it was time for something or the other again, and Rambler settled down till the rain let up enough for him to drive home.

He was still seeking that elusive story. He was also seeking that pretty girl. And he was definitely seeking to alleviate the restless feeling within.

Sunday! He had driven home in the rain the previous day. Today, it was still pouring. Chettan and Chethathi Amma had decided to brave the church and Rambler went with them. He walked and they went on the motorcycle—that was far easier than the car. It was not a very large church. Rambler thought of the beautiful, ancient Anglican Church that Alapuzha was proud of and decided to visit that as well. He did not communicate this to his brother and sister-in-law; he was not sure how they would take it. Chettan seemed to disapprove of his very existence, he felt.

'Chettan, will go around and meet Santhosh', he informed him.

'Meen curry for lunch, Johny!' His Chethathi encouraged him to return home to lunch with the promise of the spicy red Kerala fish curry.

He went to Santhosh's home, and was informed that he was at Thiruvnanthapuram and would return after two days. Rambler unconsciously walked towards the coir colony, as he had begun to call it. There was no one about on a Sunday. He went back home a little disappointed.

His brother did not have much to say to him. Earlier, when he was younger, Chethathi Amma would tease him about marriage. Then he left, seldom visited, and refused all marriage proposals that they sent. He travelled so much that his mail often returned undelivered or simply got lost. She did not broach the subject again, wondering if he was gay. *'These writer types are so different, no?'* she often thought to herself. Now she spoke of desultory domestic events.

All topics of conversation exhausted, he firmly declined to watch a Malayalam film on TV and withdrew to the verandah.

The blue screen emerged like an old friend and the good old QWERTY felt like a comfortable hug. Facebook. Madame Sadhana Vaze was going on about flash fiction and something or the other. He did not care.

I don't need this. Just a good subject. And some sex.

He thought of yesterday's pretty girl—he was pretty sure she would not jump into bed with him, but it was a pleasant thought.

Johny was not promiscuous, although he had had his share of women. Several encounters with many women, but affairs with none—he just had not stayed long enough. And falling in love—how did one even do that?

'I am not the settling kind. Chettan is the one who will carry forward the family,' he thought, thinking of his two nephews away at boarding school.

Mind, completely driven by a feeling below his waist, swung back to the pretty girl. What was she doing in that coir place, anyway? She looked so corporate. Medium height, fair-skinned, thick curly hair (children born to them would be able to start their own wig factory!) that she wore tied up in a tight bun—not loose and oily and damp like most Malayali women. She'd worn a half sari—tradition-turned-outmoded-turned-modern again, thanks to Deepika Padukone and *Chennai Express*. Bollywood's *Chennai Express* was a Hindi film about Tamilians, with a Tamilian cast barring the lead pair, and that seemed to work very well with the folks down south. This was what he roughly gathered from online reviews of the film. The bottom line was that the half sari was back. He thought of the girl in the half sari.

'Let's do something better', he told his laptop and he began studying the coir industry in Alapuzha. He had to have something to say to the girl when he went chasing after her tomorrow. Again, he was humbled by Google's impressive knowledge of the establishment of the formal coir industry in 1935, the massive employment in the decade that followed, the Travancore Labour Association and its eventual leftist leanings. The coir industry now needed a leg up, in order to boost the Kerala economy—the tourism industry was well and truly exhausted.

The Coir Act, 1965, had recognised the need to diversify their products and to tap the domestic market. If Kashmiri products reached Kanyakumari, why could Kerala not reach Kashmir?

And there's no dearth of raw material, thought Rambler. The backwaters yielded prodigious quantities of green husk, besides making transportation very easy.

'Kerala's waterways are as good as the European ones', said Google; he was really proud of that.

There is so much to do here. For once he sympathized with Chettan's viewpoint.

Young Malayalis simply vanished abroad for work, leaving the economic well-being of the state in the hands of the aging population. Keralite nurses, both male and female, were found all over Europe and the Arab nations. Other shop-floor-level workers as well, mostly male. Money lured young boys away from college education. They earned in dollars and dirhams, sent money home, sold or renovated ancestral property, converted agricultural land into non-agricultural (citing lack of labour as the prime reason); this exacerbated the problem of the neglected natural resources. Land needed care. Human resources, the young children, had to be trained from school onwards to assume responsibility for their state, especially one with as rich a potential as Kerala.

He turned off the laptop and simply sat back, breathing in the smells and the sounds. Dampness, primarily and the perfume of the rain-drenched grass! And insects, at least six different types, he was sure, judging by the variety of sounds he could hear. He used to be able to name the insects, as a child; now he had forgotten. The rain had stopped, only for a little while of course, but it was too squelchy to walk anywhere. And, it was dark.

The Changing Face of Alapuzha

Alapuzhan Anecdotes. Alapuzhan Accounts?

Alapuzha Historiette—too way out.

Rambler tested these titles on his tongue before discarding them. He had to write a story—it had to be fiction. But he was abuzz with ideas for an article, maybe several articles, even a book. He had suddenly fallen in love with his homeland again.

Dinner was a pleasant affair, as if his excitement, this new heady sense of belonging—Alapuzhan rhapsody, he called it—had communicated itself to his brother.

Rambler fell asleep that night with a smile on his face, half reaching out for the pink flutter of the half sari.

* *

Days passed, and so did Ruchi's attempts at writing a story. Several drafts decorated the back pages of old notebooks; 300 words, 416 words, and even 696 words. That was the farthest she had gone, counted it more times than the word count itself, it seemed.

She didn't want the job at the garment shop now. They paid just 15,000 each month. It would take her more than a year, she calculated, to make Rs. 2,00,000. Strangely, though, her mother was quite keen for her to take up a part-time job, nearby. *Choti-moti naukri* was how she put it. This meant that Ruchi could lend a hand in the household tasks, more to learn the ropes and get ready for marriage than to really be of use to mother. Long practice had created an efficient system that Ruchi's 'training' actually disrupted. But a mother had to do her duty.

Ma ka toh farz hai—Mrs Sharma good-naturedly did her duty to train her daughter for marital life.

In fact, neighbours were asking whether Ruchi would work or get married. And since Ruchi showed no signs of working, her mother's gambit, when she went downstairs to buy vegetables, was to say that she was relaxing at her mother's for a period, before she eventually tied the knot. (*Must remind Sharmaji to start looking for grooms*, she thought.)

The ladies of Meera Apartments, Phase II, were talking about the problems of 401. Nikhil Ahuja's young wife was going through a difficult pregnancy, her mother and her sister had come over in turns to look after her, but none of them could stay for any longer. Nikhil's own mother was too old and too far away to travel. And Nikhil was saving his leave for a real emergency. They wanted someone to be in the house for a few hours, fetch and carry for the young patient; more importantly, cook a meal and feed it to young Aryan when he returned from nursery school.

An idea was developing, fast and furious in Mrs. Sharma's head. She shot out a few questions.

'*Haan*, bedpan *hai*, but, emergency *ke liye*. Namrata can go to the bathroom on her own', answered Mrs.Verma of 402, the self-appointed spokeswoman on the issue, when Mrs. Sharma probed further.

'How much would they pay?'

'They don't want a trained nurse because there is no need, and they are so costly. Just someone who can care for the son. Nikhil prepares breakfast, and they order a dabba every night, although that is not every good. Of course, I send over food, too.

'Yes, but how much?'

'Oh, maybe 400 for four or five hours. Why?'

'Oh, Ruchi is looking for something not far from home, for a few months.'

* *

'Are you crazy, Ma?' screamed Ruchi.

Mrs Sharma shushed her husband's 'Don't talk to your mother like that' and continued excitedly, 'Five hundred per day, six hours a day. I bargained. Twelve to six. Nikhil comes home by eight, they can be alone for two hours, he said. And you don't have to cook there. I will make something nice for Aryan every day, and you can just take it upstairs when he comes. It will be good, Ruchi. And you don't have to travel. See how far people have to go for work in Mumbai. You will be right here and you have free time in the morning. And on Sunday, you don't have to go. It's better than that shop, where you have to stand for eight hours, walk or take an auto, carry your dabba, or spend money each day. Here you will not spend anything.

'And it's only for five months. Namrata's mother is coming one month before the delivery.'

'Five hundred times twenty-six times five. That's 65,000', she calculated swiftly on her mobile.

'OK, Ma. But I am keeping my money.'

The fleeting pain in her parents' eyes went unnoticed, as the family fell to making plans. Ruchi would begin the very next day, she informed Nikhil on the society intercom. She would collect the key from 402 and let herself in, by twelve with a dabba for Aryan, so Namrata would not have to get up. Aryan had to be washed and changed, and then fed. That was the toughest because he was either too hungry, or sleepy or excited about something that had happened in his nursery school. Then Namrata had the chapatis (fresh ones supplied by 402) with bananas and milk, and slept, and 'hopefully Aryan would also sleep with her', Nikhil had said. That would be her free time, in the afternoon. She could watch TV with the volume turned down low, but not before Aryan had fallen asleep. She also had to answer any phone calls; there were hardly any, because most people called Namrata on her cell phone. Aryan woke up around five, had milk and biscuits, and went downstairs to play. Could Ruchi quickly make Namrata a cup of tea (with biscuits—acidity had to be avoided at all costs) and go down with Aryan and watch over him as he played in the society compound? At six, she could take him up, leave him with his mother, and then go home. This was the routine Ruchi would have to get used to.

Ruchi was eager and excited when she woke up the next morning. She liked new beginnings. She helped her mother prepare breakfast *and* lunch. She bathed leisurely in the tiny bathroom and her mother had to bang on the door to remind her to save some water for the rest of the day. Jeans and T-shirt, *the hip nanny*, she thought dreamily. She picked up her bag (mobile, deodorant, lip balm, hanky, some money, notepad, and pencil because she hadn't forgotten about that short story thing) and Aryan's dabba and headed upstairs. Feeling important and cool, she took the key from 402 and let herself in.

Namrata looked pale. Ruchi had met her a few times downstairs when *she* had watched Aryan play around in the evenings. They had often nodded absently to each other. Ruchi had thought it boring to associate with married women, however young or old, and Namrata was too wrapped up in living for her husband, child, and household. Now, they exchanged hellos and Namrata repeated whatever Nikhil had told her over the phone yesterday.

'Go down, Ruchi, it's time for his auto.'

'Will he come with me?'

'Call me if there is a problem, I will come to the window. *Vaise*, we have told him.'

Aryan came up without a fuss and that was the beginning and end of Ruchi's happiness for the day.

He wouldn't let her help him undress, and his mother couldn't help him undress. He wanted to sit on his mother's lap while Ruchi undressed him. Several tears and some screaming later, finally they arrived at a compromise. He stood on his parents' double bed next to where his mother was lying; Namrata stroked his legs as Ruchi changed him. No bath, today. Ruchi could just get him to wash his face and hands.

Lunch with TV cartoons. Luckily, the TV was in the bedroom, and with his mother's tired encouragement, he gobbled down the alooparatha, ignoring her injunctions to 'chew, *beta*'. Ruchi stood by, hungry for her own lunch, but mindful that Namrata had to have her chapatis and bananas and milk. That done, mother and son settled down with the TV on (Aryan simply would not let go of the comfort of the cartoons).

'He's become really *ziddi* in the past month. I'll switch off the TV once he is asleep. You go and rest outside.'

Ruchi had her mother's alooparatha with the curds that she had kept to cool in Namrata's fridge, and then simply fell asleep on the couch. When she woke up, it was a quarter to five and all was quietness with the mother-son duo. Should she wake them? She made tea for herself and Namrata, and gently woke her.

'Shall we wake Aryan?' she whispered.

'Yes . . . I'll start. It's time to wake him up now.'

Aryan woke up, did pee-pee, and rushed downstairs to play. Namrata thought about positioning herself by the window but gave up the idea. Ruchi left her tea unfinished to run downstairs with the key—the key that would unlock and unchain his little bicycle with the trainer wheels, which he hadn't ridden since Sunday. Ruchi watched him go round and round the building. She wished she had thought to bring her bag with its mobile and notepad, but Namrata had just rushed her downstairs. The deodorant and lip balm with which she had intended refreshing herself also languished upstairs.

She called out to Aryan at six. He ignored her. Ten minutes later, he declared himself hungry and wanted to go up. Ruchi grabbed him before he could change his mind. She locked up the precious bicycle and they both ran upstairs.

'Maggi, Maggi, Maggi.'

Ruchi went into the kitchen and made his Maggi noodles before Namrata could even voice a request.

'Do you need anything, Namrata?'

Descending those eighteen steps to her flat downstairs was the most exhausting journey of her lifetime, Ruchi felt. Her nerves had never felt this frazzled. Never before had she felt so completely involved. She ate quietly, and slept early. The short story and Rs. 200,000 popped up in her tired brain just before it shut down for the night.

* *

Epistolary romance! That was what it was called. People pouring out their innermost feelings—intimate outpourings—in letters! There was so much passion there. She remembered the Amar Chitra Katha comics that she had read. Vignettes from Indian mythology. Shakuntala. Her friend Anusuya (or was it Priyamvada) brings her a lotus leaf and she inscribes her feelings for King Dushyant on it. *And I think there was a letter in the romance of Urvashi and Pururavas as well. It meant so much to people, once upon a time.*

rembr d tym whn u kisd me so hard in the car, bruised my lip nd then we went to med stor for antiseptic?

ENTER

my lips were a red blotch nd u cald me orangutan?'

ENTER

For months after that, orangutan had evoked reminiscent laughter.

    * *

Gulmohur Palace
26th August 1968

My dear Prince R,

You do realize that even a glance of yours makes me tingle so? And then to hold me so close, and the caress of your thumb! No one noticed, and all the while, you were nodding politely to the other waltzers! Oh, how cruel! And then you left me with that look . . . again! And danced with the elegant lady in the rich blue brocade sari (the one who had worn red the last time)! Does no one else have to do duty dances?

Yours aggrieved,

Arunima Devi

* *

Udai Palace
30th August 1968

My dear princess,

Arunima, forgive me for the delay in replying. I was caught up with some urgent matters of state.

How can you say I was being cruel? Just knowing you are in the same room does strange things to me. Even if I danced with the lady in the blue brocade, I had eyes only for the one in pink silk that matched her cheeks and her lips.

I remain

Yours ever,

Raghubir Singh

   * *

Monica looked for a sign and got none. Resigned, but not really depressed. What could she expect, after so long? Anil was in the study after dinner and came to bed long after she fell asleep.

lovd it whn we lay in bed holdng each othr all nyt, nakd. then feel cold nd dress nd cuddl agn

ENTER

lovd it when a noise outside woke us at 3AM, we had tea nd slept agn . . . aftr a quickie

ENTER

* *

Gulmohur Palace
1st Sept

Dear Prince R,

Raghubirji

My dear father has also had to travel to Himachal in haste. He could not arrange for us three sisters to travel with him at such short notice.

The venerable old Kaushalya Devi, unmarried cousin of Prince Aditya Singh, has graciously agreed to move into Gulmohur Palace for the period, to act as chaperone.

Dare I suggest we meet?

Yours only,

Arunima

  * *

Udai Palace
1st Sept

Arunima, my dear love

Kaushalya Devi is not very old, you are very young. She is just about forty, I am told.

Do you think it would behoove me to call on you when your father is not there? Let us wait, my dear.

Yours,

Raghubir

* *

Udai Palace
6th Sept

Arunima, my dear,

Are you perhaps annoyed with me? Believe me, it caused me tremendous pain to refuse your sweet request, or was it a command?

Apart from the matter of propriety, there were urgent matters of the state.

I hear that your dear father has returned and no doubt, you would have heard something about it from him. There have been rumblings about the abolition of the privy purses given to the royal families of princely states. That has serious repercussions, hence we were all required to attend to the political affairs of the state, contest elections, earn our place as rulers. But do not trouble your pretty little head over it.

I intend inviting your esteemed father to a rally that I shall be addressing on the 8th of Sept. I leave it to

you, my devious little minx, to be there with him.
Wear pink.

Yours only,

Raghubir

* *

wakn up in midl of nyt, you hard agnst me . . .

ENTER

Then Monica's phone blinked the arrival of a message.

Q: Why do women like to have sex with the lights off?

A: They can't stand to see a man have a good time!

She smiled at her phone. Some response at last!

Blink again.

What's a condom and a coffin got in common?

A: They both hold stiffs but one is cumin and one is going!

OK, so he was biting! Now she would play hard to get.

* *

Gulmohur Palace
9th Sept

My dear Prince Raghubir,

I think I now understand the problem you spoke of, although it was a little difficult to understand the local dialect. My dear father was a little surprised, but not displeased at what he called my premature interest in politics. Then he corrected himself to say that perhaps it was not premature after all; any prince whom I married would require my involvement in affairs of the state.

Did you like my pink lehariya sari? I ordered it from the bazaar of Jaipur. I custom ordered the pure silver zari work for myself.

When will we meet next, I wonder?

Only yours,

Arunima

* *

Gulmohur Palace
11th Sept

My dear Prince Raghubir

Not hearing from you fills my heart with dread. Now that dear Father is back, could you not call on us? Soon we shall leave for Himachal, after the first flush of the polo season.

My dear father is also thinking of my marriage, I overheard him speak to the Diwan. Does that not bother you?

Only yours,

Arunima

* *

Monica's phone blinked again.

A redhead tells her blonde stepsister, "I slept with a Brazilian . . ." The blonde replies, "Oh my God! You slut! How many is a brazilian?"

Monica smiled and did not reply.

Her phone blinked again.

What's the difference between light and hard? A: You can sleep with a light on.

When Monica did not tap-tap in reply, it went sadly off.

* *

Gulmohur Palace
13th Sept

My dear Prince

You have made me so happy. But how mean of you to tease me and send the invitation to dear father without informing me. Of course, we will be delighted to attend dinner at Udai Palace. What colour would you like me to wear?

Yours only,

Arunima

* *

Udai Palace
13th Sept

My beloved Arunima,

I'd love to see you in red.

Yours,

Raghubir

* *

Monica finally relented.

Sex is like a misdemeanour, the more I miss it, da meaner I get.

ENTER

Q: When is a man most intelligent, before, after or during sex?

A: During sex cuz he's plugged up to the knowledge source=:)

ENTER

Now her phone blinked.

I feel your every curve is printed on my palms.

Monica laughed out loud. Clumsy man!

* *

Gulmohur Palace
15th Sept

Dear Prince R,

Thank you for the utterly delightful dinner party. I thank your gracious wife, Radhika Devi, as well, for being such a wonderful hostess and making us feel at home.

Now it all makes sense. Your refusal to call on us makes sense. You are married. How did I not see that?

Although, I must aver that your marital status does not change my feelings for you in any way. I would be happy to be the junior queen. It would not be such a bizarre thing, would it?

My dear father, I have reason to believe, would not have any objection to this . . . I have heard him tell my old dai that he said I needed to marry a mature man.

I am confused. Do you not love me? Is that not the only thing that matters?

I will stroll in the Gulmohur Palace gardens after dark today. Please meet me. I will have to enter the palace no later than 8 p.m.

Yours,

Arunima Devi

* *

Udai Palace
15th Sept

My dear Arunima,

Your wish is my command.

Yours ever,

Raghubir Singh

* *

Gulmohur Palace

15th Sept

My beloved Raghubir,

Thank you for honouring my request. I must confess that having you pop out from behind a bush in the Gulmohur Guards uniform was surprising as it was exciting. I thought my heart would burst when you pulled me back and kissed me. It was my first, my dear prince. And I am glad it was you. Oh, that it could always be you!

I am grateful that you explained in person why we could not marry. Yes, I do agree that marriage requires much more than love. In these uncertain political times, you would not be able to support two wives. I also understand your obligation to your family, your young son. I would expect no less from a man of your stature.

That half hour in the garden will remain etched in my memory for ever more. Nor would I ever be able to forget your embrace, my bosom against your chest, your breath on mine and your kisses . . .

I know that you love me and that is enough.

Will I ever see you again?

Yours truly and forever,

Arunima Devi

* *

Udai Palace
16th Sept

My dear little Arunima,

My very own love. This would be my final missive. Do always remember that you will always hold a special place in my heart. Whenever I miss you, I shall close my eyes and think of you in my arms.

I shall, with a heavy heart, destroy all your sweet letters to me, so they do not fall into the wrong hands. You would, perhaps, want to do the same with mine?

I thank you, my little darling, for making it easy for me to carry out my obligations.

I remain

Yours forever,

Raghubir.

* *

Himadri Palace
Chail
Himachal Pradesh
1st February 1969

Dear Prince Raghubir Singh Ji

It is with great joy that I announce the marriage of my eldest daughter Arunima Devi with Prince Angad Singh of Patiala on the 14th day of April 1969.

The schedule of the ceremonies and festivities would be sent subsequently.

This early communication is to ensure that you keep yourself free to attend and to bless the young couple.

Yours faithfully,

Raja Bir Singh

Letters were good. The doorbell pealed and she ran to open the door. Monica and Anil faced each other, each sensing the fire in the other. Messages on cell phones were good too . . .

* *

Was this a mistake? At nearly 75, to attempt such tomfoolery? His course mates in Dehra Dun, or anywhere else in the country, were grandfathers many times over. They lived peacefully with their wives (if they were still alive) and visited their children abroad or wherever they were. A lot of them he knew, were hooked on to the Internet, they exchanged emails that consisted chiefly of military or political issues and dirty jokes. He enjoyed them too. He had brought his laptop along with him to Mussoorie, but was unable to connect to the Internet. He had contemplated writing his memoirs, defying the small voice in his head that asked 'For whom?'

Should he start writing his memoirs and then convert them into a story? It had to be fiction, Raghav had said. He could easily write about the countless brave jawans and officers he had served with. A cup of tea would help him think; half a cup, else he would have to keep interrupting his work to go to the bathroom. He got up and poured himself some tea from the thermos on the small makeshift dining table. He was surprised to discover that his hands were shaking. He settled down with the cup and let his mind wander over the soldiers he had known.

June 1962.

'Jai Hind, sir!' His orderly, who had just entered his bachelor's quarters with a mug of the customary wake-up tea, saluted smartly.

'Jai Hind, Jai Hind' he had said proudly, careful to return the salute with the merest stiffening of shoulders. He had just been commissioned into 13 Kumaon Regiment a week ago. Ram Lal had been assigned as his orderly, also called batman in those days, now called *sahayak*. In addition to the delicious hot tea, shiny black OPs (the Oxford pattern shoes), crisp olive-green uniforms, belt buckles that would put the most expensive mirror to shame—these were Ram Lal's valuable contributions to his young officer. Ram Lal did his job diligently and saw to it that his sahib was always well turned out and lacked nothing.

He knew when the young sahib had had a drop too many, and in that case, nimbupani would be produced before tea. And if the young sahib swore and refused to have it, he would gently coax him and make him have it anyway. No one minded a little swearing those days. Orderlies and officers were practically like brothers, albeit one privileged and the other not so (and no one would dream of crossing that boundary). They spent so much time together, away from their families. It was not unheard of, when the officer retired, for his orderly to continue to live with the family and look after them. The bonds remained long after the two individuals died.

Ram Lal! Little did he know that later that year, he would be sent to the Chinese border, in active combat and lose the devoted sepoy Ram Lal to a stray bullet.

He remembered the cold, harsh mountain passes that October night. Everyone had retired for the night, except for the men on duty. Ram Lal had served his dinner and then stood by. Or that's what he had thought. When dinner was done, he called out to him and was surprised not to find him within calling distance. Someone had cleared his plates away, and Vikram, who was officiating as commander of the little *tukdi* issued orders that Ram Lal was to be found and asked to report to him. An hour later, he was told that Ram Lal was dead. For some reason, maybe because he was destined to die, he had gone a little distance away from the camp (war played tricks on people's minds). A bullet had blown away his face.

Young Vikram had cried heedlessly at the meaninglessness of it all—at the sight of his devoted helper lying bloodied and dead. Then he had wiped his tears very fast, arranged for the body to be carried down to headquarters, and led his men from the front. He remembered the orders from headquarters. The Chinese were not supposed to have attacked so soon, but they did. And in huge numbers, they entered through Aksai Chin and Arunachal Pradesh. The Namti plains were awash with the blood of Indian soldiers.

His cheeks were wet. The lonely old man sat before his cooling tea and cried like a baby. At 1 p.m., when Bhado brought in lunch, he was surprised to see Dadaji lying fully clothed on the bed, not sleeping, not smiling, not crying, just blank. He gathered himself, when he saw Bhado, but ate poorly. He left him presently with a concerned *'Aap aaraam karo, dadaji. Kal likh lena, ji.'*

At 5 p.m., Dadaji was nowhere to be seen, and he did so love his evening chai! Wherever could he be? The devoted Bhado loitered around, wondering which path he had walked off on. He positioned himself at the U-turn of the road and asked people coming uphill and going downhill, if they had seen the old man. No one had. It was getting dark and Bhado was getting worried . . . a car stopped and Vikram emerged with Raghav.

Raghav stayed to dinner, Bhado bought some food from a nearby Chinese restaurant, and they talked. Vikram rambled on about his days in the army and his voice wobbled several times. A concerned Raghav asked if Bhado could sleep there but Vikram would have none of it. 'I am old, not helpless.'

The next morning, much refreshed by Bhado's ministrations, Vikram settled himself at the freshly smartened writing table. His talkathon yesterday had taken the edge off his misery, and he did not feel quite so lonely, only a little hemmed in by the rock face he could see from his window. He longed to see bright blue open sky.

'Not possible anywhere in India during the rainy season. Don't be an ass, Vikram,' he admonished himself.

But try as he might, he could not write! He reminisced about his own life. His wife had had to fend for herself so very often, because of his field postings. She had sometimes stayed on at the separated family accommodation provided by the army at various stations, but that was later when Abhay had started schooling; when he was younger, she would come home to Dehra Dun, to her parents. He would rush home even if he got a few days' leave and they would wait eagerly for the night. Over a period, they had gotten so used to being apart and had to work a little at knowing each other again, each time they met. They had had a pleasant life, especially after he retired, with nothing to upset them, barring the death of their son. When Reema died, they had been good friends, dependable and devoted companions.

He missed her; he missed the familiarity that was her. He also missed the asinine life of Dehra Dun that he had escaped from, but he was determined to stay here for the period he had rented the little flat.

Too embarrassed to turn to Raghav again today, Vikram sat at his table, somewhat morose. It was as if Raghav had divined his need and he turned up, with his laptop. He checked his mail (they had to use the Tata Indicom dongle here, BSNL connections did not reach into rock faces) and invited Vikram to check his. They had a good time laughing over the dirty jokes sent by Vikram's septuagenarian course mates. They also watched Sadhana Vaze's video on Facebook, but it took ages to buffer and Vikram could not get the half of it.

However, Raghav had gleaned enough to tell him that there were five smaller prizes of Rs. 20,000 each. 'If you win even that, you can go to Mumbai in October. That would be a nice change, an adventure.'

They discussed story ideas. Vikram opened his heart out to Raghav—personal and professional trials and tribulations! How life in the army had been stranger than fiction and no one cared about it very much!

For instance, the *sahayaks* were not to be seen in the same light as domestic servants. The officer's code book listed them as orderlies who would look after the personal needs of the officer, including his weapon. This left the officer to train his mind and body, in readiness to strategize and take exemplary decisions in times of war and peace. Some of the 'lady-wives' did not understand this, when they married.

'They would ask the *sahayaks* to do all sorts of jobs, including running their bathwater. Now, tell me—he is a man, without his family for so long. And here is his sahib, enjoying himself with the memsahib, sometimes within his earshot. And when the sahib is not there, memsahib is asking him to go into her bathroom and draw out the bathwater.

'The poor bugger just raped her. Or tried to. He molested her. He was thrashed. Court-martialled.'

'Why is that wrong?'

'Raghav, he has a family in the village. Maybe they have farmland and don't depend financially on him. But what does he tell them? Why was he sent home? There are others in the army, from his village. The reason for his dismissal will soon be known. Many may think that the woman asked for it, but his dismissal, per se, would always be a disgrace.'

'This could become your story!' Raghav said enthusiastically.

Raghav's morning visit had stretched into an early drinks and dinner evening. Vikram swilled his Scotch on the rocks around his mouth and reached for a leg of tandoori chicken.

'Maybe, but it is too close. Happened with someone I knew. They would know I am talking about them.' His dentures formed a white grin.

'*Sochte hain,*' Vikram agreed to think about it.

Later, Bhado came to clear the dinner dishes and heard Dadaji retching in the bathroom. Vikram took a while coming out, cleaning up after himself in the bathroom. He felt weak and quietly drank the warm water Bhado had thought to bring up in his thermos, for the night. He did not sleep that night, his stomach burning. He kept sipping water and kept going to the bathroom. When Bhado came by in the morning with tea, Vikram requested some warm milk instead. He was weak and lay in bed some more. Eventually he got up and bathed and changed. But he could not sit at the table and reclined, instead, on his bed with the newspapers. He had to be woken up for lunch and again for tea.

Bhado turned up with warm, semi-liquid *khichri* for dinner and insisted on sleeping there that night. He ended up staying the next three days, because Vikram developed an infection that gave him fever and cramps. When he was better, Raghav drove him back to Dehra Dun, Bhado in tow. Raghav had haggled with Bhado's wily father and sent him to Dehra Dun in lieu of the remaining rent. He would return when Vikram was completely recovered.

* *

'Nirbhaya', she Googled. It gave her the newspaper coverage of the grim gang rape. *Landmark verdict of a death sentence, since it was the rarest of the rare cases.* She remembered reading in the papers, for at least two weeks, exactly how it was done, how the school bus was misappropriated by the lust-drunk men—all the gory details, making newspaper readers and TV viewers shudder. People had gotten really careful after that. And perhaps for the first time, so many people had come out to protest against it. People were scared, aware, and angry.

The first time that dental evidence was admitted in a case of rape. The bite marks on the victim's body were identical with the dental impression of one of the rapists. *The juvenile one? Must check.*

The government also did its bit and started a Nirbhaya Fund to help women in distress. A popular actor was the face of a TV campaign (and naturally he must have waived his fee for this) about *asli mard*—a real man was not one who used force; he was one who protected women. Everywhere, there was propaganda about the evils of rape, how men have to be trained since boyhood to respect women and so on. At the Rajinder College, there was a signature campaign against the rape, but she had no idea what they eventually did with those charts containing a million signatures.

Once the victims were booked and the trial went underway, the public voice had muted, she recalled, even as fresh rape cases were reported in the paper. Two or three every day! Little girls, as young as 4, raped by a neighbour they knew. A boy of fourteen trying to violate a younger girl. Women in suburbs were suddenly reporting a rape a day. Was this just happening in the illustrious capital or all over the country, or the world?

There ought to be a khap even for this. These people are so protective, and possessive about their women. How do they even get raped? And what do they do after that? Is she accepted or discarded?

Were there greater number of rapes happening or were just more of them coming to light?

With the Phantom's protection, a beautiful woman clad in the finest jewels may walk in the jungle safely at midnight—old jungle saying, from the famous Phantom stories, published by Indrajal Comics. *Where were they, these days? Never heard of Indrajal Comics anymore.* Her mind returned to the task at hand.

How do I construct the story? First, decide the subject. Urban rich girl or street-side urchin? Or, how about public justice in a small community that has neither the time nor the money to approach the judicial system? Or, shall I write about the rape survivor's rehabilitation? Conviction of the rapist ... um, it would take a courtroom scene, and these must be authentic, with the proper terms and stuff. Where's the time? she thought as she wound up her session and got ready for the day.

On her way to college, she was reminded of a news item she had read somewhere. Probably in Haryana, it was. A woman was raped by her father-in-law. The panchayat declared that now she was his woman, and her husband relinquished all rights on her. No one asked her. Shuddering at the thought, Maya plunged into her classroom and forgot everything else.

Teaching the nuances of the auxiliary verbs to students, who rarely spoke English in the classroom, never outside it, was a demanding task. A frustrating day—electricity bill to pay (she must remember to go in for the online facility. But that was not without its dangers—what if all her money got siphoned off? She had precious little.) From there, it was a short easy step into her favourite nightmare—balancing her shoestring budget and factoring in her little needs and desires.

She needed to get on with that story; she had to make it work. But not today, she hadn't touched her NET books for over a week, and now she was nervous. *After all, this story and everything will not happen to everyone. There is only one prize. All of us can't get it. Success in the NET exam is also not assured, but seems more doable.*

The week passed in a blur—college, cooking, cleaning, cramming for NET, visiting ailing aunt at the other end of town because the aunt's daughter called her up to gently remind her how they had helped her out when her father was sick. The rains made most other absences at family gatherings excusable, thank God. The rains were not heavy, but oppressive enough for the user of public transport. The one advantage of living in a megalopolis as sprawling as Delhi was that people completely understood formidable distances, seasonal compulsions, and traffic congestions.

A little more research on Mr Google, my friend. Nope. There were other rapes listed, but not the one she remembered, where the woman was forced by the panchayat to now cohabit with the father-in-law.

Can't just write anything without knowing the facts, even if it is fiction . . . her thoughts trailed off.

She put out the garbage, made herself a cup of tea, and sat down again.

She remembered the promos of a book that had appeared in Facebook a while ago, Manoj and Babli—A Hate Story; the author's name had stuck—Chander Suta Dogra.

It was about khap 'justice', I think. What if the khap makes a compassionate decision, delivers a compassionate verdict, in favour of the woman? That would be lovely and different, and perhaps, truly fiction. She smiled at the impossible.

She looked through her Nirbhaya research again.

What about her boyfriend, who was forced to witness all this and could not help? He must feel guilty as hell. And so emasculated. Was he perhaps undergoing psychiatric treatment? Shall I write from that angle?

A phone call and another cup of tea later, she began writing.

* *

Maria's Story

It was a pretty day in Colva. I was at home, cleaning. It was a favourite task ... very satisfying. And that year we had had a good tourist run right till June. Now the house was empty, and although it was raining outside, it was the only time to turn over the beds, air them, thoroughly clean and dry the linen under the fans, scrub the rooms and bathrooms with Annie the maid.

We were doing well, and I hoped that one day, we would be able to engage professional cleaners at least once a year. I knew there was a small company at Colva—Sunshine Cleaners. They had these cheerful bright yellow uniforms, with a red sun on the pocket. They did the big resorts. They were still too expensive for us, but maybe one day . . .

But we must look at our accounts again and see if we can build a small drying room. The backyard did get crowded in the tourist season; tourists were so demanding these days and the linen had to be very, very clean, changed at least twice a week. Jerry was thinking of heaters or fans or something, which would dry out the wash in double-quick time. We already had a washing machine that worked round the clock in tourist season. No dishwasher, I needed extra help for the dishes, and if it wasn't there, I just did it. Jerry helped if he was not busy with something else.

Right now, it's manageable. I can dry the wash in the empty rooms—all three bedrooms are empty. And probably will remain so for three or four months. Maybe Jerry's brother and his family will come for a vacation. Or Sandra and her family will. Let's see.

I finished the job of hanging out the wash on the makeshift lines, and went to the kitchen to make lunch. No fish today. I was making egg curry and rice. Put in two extra eggs . . . it would go for dinner as well.

The doorbell rang and I saw a dripping girl with straw-coloured hair smiling at me. She was tall, really tall, and broad, almost as broad as Jerry. And she had very white skin that looked opaque. So different from our brown, glowing Goan skins! She spoke with a heavy accent; we were used to that by now.

'I am Natasha. This is a home stay? Can I stay?'

I did not have the heart to say that we would like a little rest from caring for guests. I told her she would have to wait while I got a room ready, and we could have lunch in the meantime. She used our bathroom to freshen up. Annie quickly got the small room ready; Natasha paid up front, for six months. Well, if our relatives came to visit, they could stay in the other larger rooms.

Natasha told us a little about herself over lunch. She was Russian, had come down to India to quietly, peacefully, and comfortably write a book. It was a novel set in Russia. 'Ironic that I have to come out of Russia to write it,' she had giggled.

Natasha was a delight. She was neat and tidy and punctual for meals, so punctual that it improved our eating habits. And she would be really relaxed and chatty over dinner. We learnt that her family was reasonably well-to-do and could take care of her for a while more, which is why she had no pressure to earn. She had grown up reading the Russian masters and wanted to write an epic in the same tradition—a grand tragic drama like Anna Karenina—a revival of sorts of the old writing, in these modern times. On the basis of a small publisher advance, she had come down to 'cheap' India to write her book.

A month passed. Natasha was like family. She would sometimes come and chat with me in the kitchen. On the days that we had to go out, she would chat with Annie; and if Annie was not there, she would cook herself a simple meal. She had learnt to eat right for the climate, so she should not fall sick. Fish and rice, prawns and rice. She drew the line at vindaloo; it was too spicy for her. But she could polish off an entire bebinca at one go.

The other people had also got used to seeing her stride about on the main street, picking up oddities, buying old books and selling hers at the BookShop, a popular second-hand bookshop. The rain did not seem to bother her much, used as she was to Russian sleet and snow.

In October, tourists started trickling in. Goa had become popular with Russians in the past two or three years and we began to see many more of them in the streets. Maybe that's where Natasha met them and became friendly with a group. She mentioned them over dinner one day. She also mentioned the name of the resort where they were staying and the name of one man—was it Alex?—with whom she was quite friendly.

Then she began spending more and more time with them. Jerry and I realized that all these months, she was probably missing her people. We were concerned that she would try to bring the man home. We did not want these lust stories happening in our home. What she did outside the home was her business. She never introduced us to Alex.

'We are not her parents, dear. Besides, if our guests choose to have someone over for the night, we can hardly object. We can only object to the visitor taking up residence', Jerry said when I pointed this out. We were prepared that the cosy family scene was ending.

But, we were not prepared for the horrifying manner in which it ended.

That day, it was a Saturday, I remember, Natasha did not come down for breakfast. It was getting late and the food was getting cold, so I carried it upstairs to her. I knocked and got no response, many times! She had not latched the door. So I just pushed it open and almost died of shock. She was lying on her bed—naked—and dead. The room had been ransacked.

I ran downstairs with the tray and yelled for Jerry. We both ran up again, I covered her body with a sheet. Jerry ran down to call the police.

The rest of the day was a nightmare. They came. Took her body for a post-mortem. There were signs of sexual intercourse, there were traces of a drug in her tissue. Probably she had died of a drug overdose. We had no idea if any of her belongings were missing; we just knew she had come in with one large suitcase and that she regularly bought things in Colva market. The police made a rough list of the things that were there.

'Whom did she meet here?' they wanted to know.

'Colva Resort, a group of Russians. I think there was a man called Alex.'

Then the second shock—that entire party had disappeared the previous night; whether they had flown back to Russia or were somewhere else in Goa was anybody's guess. It would take a while to track them down to their addresses in Russia. The problem was complicated and had grown beyond the powers and capabilities of the Colva police. The matter went to Panjim, the capital of Goa, and would eventually involve the embassy.

We lost track. The body was, however, still at Colva, temporarily kept on blocks of ice. No one knew where to send it. We offered to take responsibility and had it cremated. We sent the ash by courier to the address Natasha had given us, God knows if it reached or who it reached.

What if some day, her parents or anyone came down asking about her? How would we face them? What would we say? That we had neither the time nor the money, nor the power to follow up the case? Oh, wrong. We had the time, because no one came to our house anymore. The tourists had stopped coming to us.

Annie had screamed hysterically and refused to clean out that room. She had also blabbed to her friends about the incident. People would come and randomly stand and stare at the house. Soon, it was used as a landmark to give directions, 'the house of the Russian girl's murder' then the shortened and more poetic version—'haunted homestay'.

That did it. We had to sell and move away. The owner agreed to let Natasha's stuff remain for a year in case someone from her family came for it. Jerry and I wanted to make a clean break, so we chose to move out of Goa. Someone suggested Pune, and we went there and tried to start afresh.

'What do you think, Jerry?'

'It's not really a story, Maria. It's real. And you have rushed the ending, dear.'

'Hmm. But I like what I have written. But, it's too short. Not even 1,500 words.'

'Add some make-believe. Make it a whodunit. Solve the case. Get out the Agatha Christies', he laughed and said.

* *

Hurried preparations had been made. Only they could not look hurried. Conference room 1 was spruced up. Luckily it was a Sunday, and the office was nearly empty, except for the people who needed to be here for the shoot today, and a couple more that were lagging behind on work or escaping from home on the pretext of work. Empty offices made the task easier.

Jay had already set up his camera. The first shot would of the banner of the Indus logo, on the conference room wall. That was already in place. Not an innovative shot, but effective. Rohan Bagade, the office boy, was dragging in a standee, from an earlier event. There was the predictable pile of books with a feather quill on top of it, and the Indus logo. He would use a soft focus so the carefully whitened-out irrelevant dates and data would not show.

Jay Kapoor loved his Sundays. He also loved his work and Meher Azam. And today was the perfect confluence of all three loves. It would be a good day.

The room was ready and Meher dispatched Rohan to arrange breakfast and coffee—breakfast from the cafe outside the office, and coffee from their very own Nescafe machine. Ramona was on her way; she did not need to be. Meher was a capable young woman, but Ramona wanted to leave nothing to chance. Meher did not resent this. She knew Ramona trusted her and relied on her, and also that sometimes she simply needed to be hands-on. And they got along well; they were good sounding boards for each other.

Ramona arrived, Sadhana also arrived. They rehearsed over coffee. The camera rolled. Sadhana sat at the desk, the Indus logo emblazoned behind her, and spoke her lines. The camera followed her as she stood up and walked a semicircle, still speaking. The first shot was over.

Sadhana declared herself unhappy with the rushes. 'I look short and wide. Maybe I should remain seated?'

'It's a movie, Sadhana ma'am, a video.' Jay was a little impatient and trying not to show it. 'There has to be movement.'

'Maybe if I walk from left to right, not right to left—I think that's my better side.'

'OK, we'll do it once more, use the same floor marks', Jay said after some thought and adjustment of cameras.

'But trust me on which take to finally use.' Jay looked at Meher and Ramona for support.

'Jay will make you look good, Sadhana. And some bits can be Photoshopped, right, Jay?'

'Yes. Let's get through this calmly and quickly, because there is a lot to be done before I ready it for broadcasting.'

They shot a few more scenes in the Indus office, minus the Indus logo. They also included shots of Sadhana holding up a copy of *Twelve Tales of Summer.*

The whole affair was a little clumsy and not quite Ramona's style—the date mix-up for instance. She would have liked the main event to be on the autumn equinox, but they had woken up too late. Then, it would have helped if some of the shoot could be done at Sadhana's place. But there was no time. Well, she would make the most of a bad thing; she could do that!

They shot the second part of the video in Jay's studio. He used his props to make it look like a cosy study. Sadhana was not pleased with the lamp Jay had placed. 'It's not feminine. And it's dreadfully dull,' she added tactlessly. Jay had ignored her and Meher's 'You'll make it look good, Sadhana' actually came out sounding sincere.

'Etch, Elaborate, Embellish' was the three-step process Sadhana was explaining—you first made an outline of the story, then you expanded each point, finally you added the details. She spoke about flash fiction. She spoke about several other writers' forums and online communities and urged the participants to join them in order to remain connected to writing, even after the competition.

'I want to see *you* on October 15,' she ended dramatically, as Jay had instructed her.

Ramona sensed that Sadhana felt she had not been treated grandly enough. She took her downstairs to the Choklit Place to soothe her nerves. Meher stayed back with Jay.

* *

Rambler made his way to coir colony the next day; he had to. He ambled in, pretending he was a wholesale dealer in coir and wanted to buy bulk quantities of products. He inspected the mats—they were made of a thin twisted rope coiled around itself to form a 1 foot by 1 foot square. Many such squares were joined to form larger mats. The beauty was that you could purchase any size you liked; they would stitch those many squares together and give it to you. 'It is nice, sar, and you can fold in any way', he was informed by one of the workers. The way he said the two *l* sounds, like he'd folded his tongue twice around the word, made it sound really foldable.

He made some random statements and looked around some more, keeping eyes peeled, ears cocked, and nose alert for sight, sound, or scent of her. The scent came first—she wore a massive amount of orange and white flowers in her hair.

'Yes, please.' Her *l* accent was much fainter than the worker's.

'How can I help?' Music!

'Johny Kutty, journalist', he said at the same time that the worker informed her that he was a wholesale dealer in coir products.

She cocked an interrogative eyebrow and he said sheepishly 'Journalist, travel writer actually. Rambler.'

It turned out that she had read an article of his in *The Lonely Planet*.

She was opinionated and articulate, was Shiny Sivadasan. She was also an IT engineer, but had given up her corporate job to return home to Kerala. 'Why?' asked Rambler, although he did not feel the question so strongly after his own ruminations last night.

'Hmm . . . many reasons. My parents want me to marry. But I don't want to marry. Not now. I like this work that I am doing.' Her hand swept around the little coir industry. 'We are Ezhavas', she continued. Ezhavas are believed to have brought coir into Kerala from Sri Lanka. Traditionally, they have had monopoly over the business. 'But now, like all other people of other castes, they are looking at better jobs outside Kerala, and abroad. Kerala is also changing. There is no one to do the physical work. Tell me, if we don't work for our state, in our state, who will?'

Her father had been a member of the Coir Board and a part of its history, its fortunes and failures. He believed, like many of his colleagues, that the coir industry needed a shot in the arm and that it was capable of delivering much more if efficiently managed. They were catering to the rising exports, for sure—their coir yarn and fibre and lawn was much in demand in even France, the fashion capital of the world. 'People abroad are appreciating, but we don't appreciate in our own country.' Shiny's charming bosom heaved in indignation and Rambler's attention slipped for the moment. She had come back to rejuvenate coir products in the domestic market. 'It takes time and effort and we need many more dedicated people to do this.'

'You are a writer, why don't you write about this in international papers? Or, even *India Today*?' If he did write a zetetic piece, it might wake up the Coir Research Institute and the Training and Design School from their slumber. *That should provide employment to hundreds of workers, and even to a few hundred research scientists. Not a bad idea,* thought Rambler on his way back home. Chetathi Amma asked him not to be late for lunch.

Rambler felt like writing Shiny's story. He need not ask her really, he could change some details. He would change her name. Even her occupation. She could be just anyone who was drawn home after a long period of being out. Like himself. But he would not change the chocolate glow of her skin.

Did Ezhavas marry outside their caste? he thought idly. *Whoa, whoa, whoa!* He stopped himself. He did not like where his thoughts were heading. While it was true he was charmed by his home state this time, like he never had been before, he did not know when he would take off again, when he would need to take off again. He had to earn his living after all, and the only way that he knew how to do it was to travel and write.

What will happen to Shiny's efforts, if everyone thinks like me?

He shrugged off the idea before it settled.

Not my problem. He checked his mail and started outlining some ideas for his next few articles, which he had decided would be on Kerala.

The next day he was back to learn more about coir and its charming, chief champion. She had also been a champion athlete at school, a sprinter. This bit of information was divulged when she proved indefatigable running up and down the coir colony, to the processing sheds and back at least twenty times a day. She worked alongside the workers, whenever needed, and managed her micro business, completely hands-on. Her athletics, at her school, Kendriya Vidyalaya Allepey, had resulted in her being sent to the Kendriya Vidyalaya, Bangalore, which was the regional training centre for girls' athletics.

That was when the 'outside' bug had bitten. She had stayed at the school hostel, grown to love Bangalore, gotten admission to a course in computer engineering. Two years of school, four years at college, and six years of the heady corporate life and she was ready to return to her roots! 'What about you?' she asked. He sketched out his life and career briefly. She listened, unimpressed.

Rambler also met her father the next day, and was fascinated at the insight he got into the whole coir affair. Initially a little awkward, when faced with the microphone in Rambler's mobile, Sivadasan was soon waxing eloquent about his favourite subject. At the end of it, Rambler had recorded 42 minutes worth of verbal wealth.

Sivadasan's office was simple and efficient, like the man himself. There was an air of briskness about that single room that sat in the midst of the idyllic greenery. He breathed deep. The smells he smelt were heady and he felt he never wanted to smell exhaust fumes again.

'The library at Alapuzha might have some old books and records. I will give reference, if you want to check and see.'

He wrote on a piece of paper and handed to over to him.

'Meet S. Achyuthan. Tell him Sivadasan has sent, he will help you.'

The Allepey Library (they had not repainted 'Alapuzha' over the 'Allepey' on that old sign yet) was decrepit (*everything important is lying neglected*), but stocked with history. Several records were in Malayalam and he bypassed them. He read letters and reports in English, all containing the details that Wikipedia could use as verifications for their citations. The cup brimmeth over. He sat right there and drafted his article. And out of it also came a powerful story.

* *

Ruchi hardly knew how the next four days went by. One day Aryan refused to come up with her and she had to carry him upstairs, screaming and kicking. Another day he refused the dal chawal her mother had cooked and she had to make him Maggi noodles again and then cool them very fast because he was really hungry and sleepy. One day he refused to go down and the next day he refused to come up.

Then, blessed Sunday!

The second week passed as fast as the first. Aryan was getting more used to her. He even let her sponge him with a wet towel while his mother stroked his leg. And he ate all of Mrs. Sharma's undoubtedly tasty lunches. Then, mercifully, he slept. Ruchi did not need her afternoon sleep so much and took the time to call her friends.

'How's the story coming along?' asked Kavita.

Ruchi had not forgotten, but simply did not have the time or the bandwidth to think about it.

Nikhil took Saturday off, so Ruchi had some extra time to herself. She made several story outlines. An ardent watcher of Hindi films would recognize the synopses of *Kuch Kuch Hota Hai, Baghban,* and *Student of the Year.* But, after the first 400 words, Ruchi simply did not know what to do.

Nikhil called on Monday morning before he left for work.

'Could you come up by 11 a.m.? The telephone *wala* is going to connect the instrument near Namrata, so she can use the intercom. Please supervise that.'

He was going to pay her for the extra hour. Ruchi did not know whether it was decent to accept the extra money. Oh, well, he wasn't paying her today! She was upstairs at 11 a.m. She noticed a small second-hand TV waiting to be mounted on the living room wall.

'That's a surprise for you, Ruchi. You can watch TV in the afternoon. The cable guys are also coming today.'

Nice start, thought Ruchi.

There was a never-ending stream of visitors—telephone guy, presswala, home delivery of grocery, and then Aryan. Some scary-looking young men asked for donation for a Gurudwara; she had just said 'Madam is not at home.' How did her own mother deal with all this? What was the security guard at the gate doing?

The cable guys came in just before 5, and Aryan had to play indoors again.

Cooking and caring for Aryan and Namrata had become second nature to her and she dealt with that and all of the above with an ease that surprised her. Only her story remained incomplete and it was already August!

Ruchi received her first month's salary with delight and tears. She had asked for cash because she had not opened a bank account yet. She had handed over the entire amount to her mother who kept it in the 'mandir', their little marble shrine above the dining table, for a few hours. Then she handed it back to Ruchi and Ruchi handed it back to her.

'*Aap se maang loongi*', she assured her mother that she would ask her for pocket money. As the sentimental tears flowed, the quiet and practical Mr Sharma suggested opening a bank account.

* *

Ruchi was at the mall with Sanjay; they were meeting after many Sundays. She was planning to tell him that they should not meet anymore. She just did not feel like it, somehow. They had very little to say to each other. Sanjay barely listened when she spoke of Namrata and little Aryan. He just seemed to be eyeing other girls. And she hardly knew what he spoke, because her mind was busy with other questions and answers.

Would Aryan miss her today? And the little heart-to-hearts she and Namrata had gotten into the habit of having? She had learnt that Nikhil and Namrata had actually fallen in love with each other, and then, for some reason, chosen a convoluted trail of common acquaintances to present it as an arranged marriage.

Once they were engaged, they had even indulged in dry sex, Namrata had coyly confessed. But she hastily advised Ruchi not to do anything, unless it was with the man she was going to marry.

'We were going to be married, na' was her reasoning.

Thankfully there were no mother-in-law recriminations; the lady was really too old to meddle with her daughter-in-law. Many other dreams the young mother had shared, how she would nurture her family and help it grow—Aryan and the little one after him: Aradhya if it was a girl, Arjun if it was a boy.

Ruchi also spoke of Sanjay, but very sketchily, giving none of the details that would give rise to censure.

At Inorbit, she and Sanjay had settled into the food court; he had left his phone with her, thrown a casual 'Check your mail' over his shoulder, as he went to get a cold coffee. Ruchi had insisted on paying for the coupons, since she was earning now.

Oh, they are on FB also, now, she thought, when she saw Indus' post on Kavita's page. She clicked on Send a Friend Message.

It was horrible having nothing much to say. Both she and Sanjay were glad to part ways after the cold coffee. Ruchi returned home and spent the rest of the evening waiting to get to work the next morning.

Oh . . . the story, she remembered suddenly. She pulled out her notes, the synopses of the many Hindi films she had watched over the years. She even knew some of the dialogues by heart. Should she use one of those?

Wonder how Kavi is getting along?

Kavi was getting along just fine, a phone call revealed.

* *

The next morning, Namrata had a guest: her brother, Rajesh.

What a name! thought Ruchi uncharitably; it reminded her of the less desirable boys in school, and of Rajesh Khanna, the handsome superhero of yesteryears, whose good looks evaporated as he got older.

'Rajesh is here for four days, Ruchi. Some work, he has.'

He reminded her of Dilip Kumar, when he was young. Sort of ordinary, and dependable. Unlike the smooth

Sanjay who wore too-tight jeans, even in the Mumbai heat.

Rajesh ran some kind of a training institute in Nanded. He was here to scout the poorer colleges for students who might want cheaper engineering diplomas at his state-of-the-art Nanak Institute. He had visions of making it a university. He stepped out each morning and Ruchi did not see him for two days. On Wednesday, she did. Ruchi was naturally attractive to men. She and Rajesh got talking after she checked her Facebook and mail on his laptop.

Mainly, he talked. And, mostly about his plans for the future. Then Namrata and Aryan woke up and they moved inside. It was good to have Rajesh around, because he took Aryan out and Ruchi was free to go home.

On the dining table, there were two letters with photographs of young men and Ruchi's heart sank. She just did not care for those chocolate boy looks, not after Sanjay. But her time was running out, she knew. Once the baby was born, and Namrata did not need her anymore, her mother's persuasion would begin in earnest. Desperately, she thought of the story and the 2,00,000, as if that would buy time with her parents.

Maybe there would be consolation prizes; she clutched at the straw.

She added a few more stilted sentences to her synopses, little realizing that she was digging for a well in many places. She was simply not able to focus her energies on one story.

Her mother asked her to look at the two photographs. She looked without enthusiasm. They were rich, and kind of cheesy good-looking; but they were ... they were just boys!

Do I want an older man?

She wondered if Namrata would die in childbirth and she would marry Nikhil and look after Aryan.

'You are sick, Ruchi!' she chided herself, thinking of Namrata's sweet face and the obvious love she and Nikhil had for each other.

I want that kind of love.

'*Milne mein to harj nahin hai*', Mrs Sharma was saying—no harm in meeting the boys. They had both already approved Ruchi's pictures.

'*Theek Hai, Ma*', she had responded automatically.

The enthusiastic mother arranged for Rohan Mehra to visit their home, sit with the family for a while, and then maybe he and Ruchi could go to Inorbit for half an hour or so. Then if they liked each other, the parents could progress the talks.

'I am meeting Rohan Mehra next Sunday', she informed Namrata, when she met her the next day.

* *

The mail from the Lit Club told her that Equinox now had a Facebook presence.

Hiya, all Writwits

Scary cheery, thought Monica.

There's good news and some more good news. You all know that the grand first prize is Rs. 200,000. The lucky winner will also get his next book (or the next three short stories) published by Indus.

And . . . there are other lucky winners. Rs. 20,000 for the next five best stories.

Pathetic.

Indus will honour the six stars at the Grande Palace, Mumbai on the 15th of Oct, 2013. We hope you will find a place there.

Meanwhile, watch this space for an exclusive video 'My Story', featuring Sadhana Vaze, winner of the Economist Crossword Book Awards 2013, for her collection of short stories—*Twelve Tales of Summer.*

Monica stretched happily; she felt like a bride. Her story was nowhere near over, *but my life story has just gotten exciting.* The cheesy messaging had stoked a forgotten fire, rekindled her romance with Anil. They had managed to shrug off the ennui and staleness that settles over every marriage when the romance is not kept simmering, or the communication not kept open. It was hard work. Like most couples, Anil and Monica had neglected their equation and focused their energies on the practical aspects—as if it was not the most practical and desirable thing in the world to get along well and enjoy the company of the person with whom you shared your home, bed, and life. Anil was doing well at work and that kept him really busy and out of the house for long spells. Monica had allowed herself to drift into the social butterfly world that had so completely consumed her and left her feeling void and empty inside. She did not intend to let that happen again.

Now, they were rediscovering each other sexually, were more accepting of each other. They fully intended to enjoy being with each other before the demons called menopause and andropause struck; the newspapers really put the fear of God into you these days, with their stream of dreary articles on the various human 'pauses'.

She was sifting through her books and reorganizing her bookshelf. Dusting, wiping, and of course, flipping open, breathing in the whiff of the old favourites. Occasionally, she would trace her name written there, in decades-old ink, along with the date of purchase.

Oh! The Passions of the Mind, she had forgotten that comprehensive biography of Sigmund Freud. She arranged all her Irving Stones together; there were three more in addition to *Passions.* She caressed the covers of her Jane Austens, the inevitable Complete Works of Shakespeare that every book lover had, and which she had not completely read. But she loved having them, and did read them when the mood took her. Why, she'd reread *Romeo and Juliet* on a whim last year, and quite enjoyed it.

The Lit Cub had introduced the newer authors like Amish Tripathi and Ashok Banker with their interpretations of the Ramayana and other mythological stories. Monica had somehow bypassed them, in favour of originals in Sanskrit, also which she had not yet read, and planned to read someday. Monica felt a little ashamed of herself and then brushed off the feeling.

'No room for negativity', she said firmly to herself.

'Let me see what I can do *now—*'

She was almost done organizing one section of the rosewood shelf. *No sense in involving myself with the housework now.* Let Sushil earn his money, ditto for the others. She realized that she was fortunate enough to not have to worry about survival and mundane chores.

A lot of women in her situation, she knew, visited Dharavi and other slums, trying to help the people there. Some could actually touch a few lives. Others were exhausted at the sheer effort and patience such projects required—they would come home, sip their chilled nimbupani or beer in AC rooms, and feel ill-used. Some of her friends were completely taken aback by the hostility they encountered amongst the slum-dwellers. The feeling of haves and have-nots was deeply ingrained in the psyche of the slum dwellers and they did not like to be made to feel small or lacking. Who the hell were these perfumed ladies? Many perfumed ladies had their clutches and handbags and mobiles stolen on these jaunts.

Mumbai is scary, thought Monica as she recalled the unattractive worldly-wise eyes of many slum children she had encountered.

Well, she would think of all that a little later. First things first.

Let's get that story done. If I win the prize money, I can at least sponsor a child's education or something, through CRY or World Vision or Akanksha. Two lakhs is a tidy sum. Even twenty thousand is not bad. And I can easily get in touch with the local arm of Akanksha in Mumbai

The story!

Let me earn that money, first, before I spend it! She smiled to herself. She took a printout and went through it. She judged herself mercilessly. *Too short, a little pretentious, also wishy—washy—not passionate enough. I need the grandeur of Rajasthan. And maybe, Arunima can stay for a polo match? Maybe she will not be so understanding about Raghubir's compulsions? I must reconcile this with her innate grace and dignity as a royal princess. And clothes. Must describe a lot of clothes.*

- *Google polo, royal matches*
- *Rajasthani royal clothes, try pix from museums?*

Monica stared at her notepad and tapped her pen thoughtfully against her head. *What else do I need?* She did not really want to write the conventional story; this epistolary romance thing was fun. *The epistles have to be pepped up.*

- *Add more letters—about the books she is reading, her activities?*
- *Add letters from other people—someone else, to Radhika Devi telling her that her husband is getting involved here? Radhika Devi could invite Arunima to tea ... um ... no—that was too much like* Zubeidaa, *the film.*
- *Formal invitations to the polo matches, invite could be in embossed format, not just text.*
- *snippets from newspaper. Would it remain epistolary in that case?*

Maybe I can construct the story using just the different types of written communication available during those times. Letters, invitations, newspaper clips, notes to secretaries, reminders, dhobi lists (really?), shopping lists, diary entries . . . of course, yesss, the diary entries can have all the details of the gorgeous dresses that Arunima sees at parties and functions and other girly things . . . yes, indeed.

Throw in a telegram for drama! Her eyes shone at the idea, at the idea of attempting something new. She remembered something.

-    *Watch Facebook video*

* *

The familiar environs of Dehra Dun lifted Vikram's spirits. Perhaps that ill-thought interlude at Mussoorie had been necessary for him to understand the value of old friends and known surroundings. Some of his friends would stop by or he would visit them. Or they would all meet at the DSOI, the Defence Officers' Institute. Vikram found a renewed interest in bridge and was soon part of a regular four. Reminiscences, were of course, part and parcel of their conversations, and Vikram and Sekhon decided to put together a collection of memoirs. They could discuss it on their walks and work on it on the non-bridge days. They needed a typist. Who could they hire?

'Vikram, want a tight skirt on your wrinkled lap, eh?' Nautiyal ribbed.

He couldn't find them a typist, but he did dig out an old Dictaphone from somewhere and Vikram began speaking into it, while they waited for a suitable typist. Sekhon declined to speak—'*angrez to tu hai*' (you are the Englishman)—he told Vikram. The Dictaphone was duly installed at Vikram's and Bhado, who had chosen to remain, recognized it as a revered object of Dadaji's.

Vikram would make his notes every morning after breakfast, revise them once during the day. At night, before going to bed, he would look at them again, visualise himself speaking into the Dictaphone, people reading all these words in a book, in a library. He would wake at 4 a.m. A sleepy Bhado would give him a cup of tea and biscuits and go right back to bed. For an hour, Vikram would gently speak his stories into the Dictaphone. Its little tapes, now a repository of untold military history, gave him the same pleasure that little grandchildren would.

Vikram was a happy man, fulfilled man. He had finally located a typist at the EBD bookstore in the Main Market. She agreed to come to his place at 8 a.m. each day, and type for an hour. She needed a computer and

Vikram had one. Bhado had come along with him for the jaunt. He used to saunter around the Paltan Bazaar for the daily household needs, but the shops around the Clock Tower were a far cry from those. They were really smart and Bhado gawked at the pretty girls and young cadets alike. Vikram took him to Ellora's and he had his fill of sweets over there.

His nephew and his family had also come over for their annual leave, and bhabhi, his sister-in-law, had stayed back. She was thinking of an old people's home. With some persuasion, he had got her to move in with him; it was the family home, after all. It was a somewhat unusual situation—the older sister-in-law making her home with her younger brother-in-law—it would have been unacceptable if they had been younger.

The old buaji was a bit of a nag, Bhado felt, especially while he cooked in the kitchen, but otherwise there was not much he had to do. Just get their medicines from the MI Room, and if he did not get it there, then from the medical store in the Main Market. Any excuse to visit the Clock Tower market! Bhado loved seeing the IMA cadets in their uniforms and expressed to Vikram his wish to join the army. Clearly, with his lack of education, he could not become an officer, but he was learning some English; Shubha, the typist, was teaching him. Bhado could aim to become a jawan, a foot soldier, but he was not sure what his date of birth was, he could be anything between 18 and 23. That was a problem. But Bhado knew Dadaji would find something for him. He was also not a matriculate, a requirement for the lesser trades in the army.

Dadaji, meanwhile, was more than happy at the progress of the memoirs.

* *

Maya was watching Sadhana Vaze sitting against the backdrop of a giant logo of Indus Publishers, talking about *Twelve Tales of Summer*, published by New Age Publishers.

Sadhana spoke of her wanting to be a writer. 'There is a story inside of everyone, and each one should write it', she insisted. She had written four books. Three of them did not do very well; a number of copies of even the first edition remained unsold. They all had been novels.

But Sadhana had believed in her stories and in her power to tell them. 'I decided to tackle my idea-demons in the short story format', she said. The result was *Twelve Tales*. Sadhana spoke briefly about the role the Internet had played in shaping her.

'People want stories, nice, interesting stories. And they want them at the click of a button.'

There were hundreds of forums where you could test the literary waters. Flash fiction, regular fiction, poetry, maybe even essays—writers shared what they wrote, and others posted comments on them. That gave you a feel about how popular your stories could become. You meander too long and your reader will mouse along to the next writer. Stories in instalments appeared on several sites. They kept reader appetite whetted and probably gave the poor writer some respite in which to spin his yarn.

'Flash fiction is a tequila shot. It has to hit just then and just so, or you lose the reader.

'Practice flash fiction. Try to write your story in about 300 words or thereabouts. There is no room for subplots here. And keep your thesaurus handy. Embellish it later, with details of people, events, and things—that is an exercise in itself—to keep it relevant and interesting.

'And for competitions such as Equinox—the name is delicious enough for me to want to write for it!' Here Sadhana had smiled.

'Do it, even if you believe you can't. Select your subject, plot their story on a timeline, and then start writing, in chunks of 50 or 100 words. *You will get there!*

'I want to see *you* on October 15.' Sadhana poked her forefinger at the screen and signed off like the encouraging mentor-friend she'd been paid to be.

It worked. Maya was encouraged. Writing up to a word count was not such a huge problem. Her commercial writing had slowly and painfully trained her to do that. She could sometimes write a 500-word load of drivel. She decided to try flash fiction. It sounded exciting. She checked out the Internet for flash fiction samples. Dismay!

They were all dark (noir, it was called, she discovered) or fantastical. *I don't know if I can write like that, or even if I want to.* She browsed some more, mulled a little more on what she could write.

She had a class to prepare for. It was vocabulary. With his signature lack of deliberation, Rajinder Khosla had decided to introduce CAT style verbal ability classes once every week. Her job was to only 'teach' the photocopied list of 20 or 30 words, with their multiple choices of synonyms, antonyms, or analogies.

A typical entry would read:

BRIEF

A.	Limited	B.	Small
C.	Tiny	D.	Short

The students had to eliminate three responses to arrive at the exact, correct synonym. As the teacher, Maya had to help them see the reasons for eliminating three options and selecting the fourth. That these tests were now available, for free, on several websites did not interest Rajinder or his students.

It did not interest Rajinder, because he charged the students extra for these 'special classes', although Maya received no extra remuneration. It did not interest the students because they could not be bothered to make that extra effort. And anyway, many of them needed the degree, *thappa* they called it, because it looked good. Majority of students would join their family businesses, poor, modest, or flourishing, whatever they might be. Few girls would actively seek an enriching career. Most would look for glamour, some for government jobs, because that also was one way of attracting a nice catch. Some bright jewels, of course, shone through the generality, and it was for the pure pleasure of teaching these learners that Maya studiously went over the vocabulary lists, referring to her dictionary, making extra notes in the margins about word origin and usage that would be of interest to the more zealous of her students.

She got up to prepare her brief evening meal. She had to resist the temptation to eat 'bread-anda' every day—quick, nutritious, and boring—and she forced herself to prepare a vegetable or a dal with roti or rice. Only on weekends did she have noodles or a pizza. When her mother was alive, she would sometimes go out with her friends for dinner, knowing her mother would take care of the evening meal for herself and Papa. Then Mama died, and she seldom left her father alone on evenings. And now she just did not feel like it.

'I have to get things back on track', she said to herself a hundred times, not quite clear what it meant—whether she meant an illustrious career, a comfortable pensionable job, or remarriage.

This weekend she would not be so lonely, she thought, pushing away her depressing thoughts. Babloo would be here, from Saturday evening through Sunday evening. The driver would drop him and pick him up from her residence on Sunday. Her son! More than two months since she had seen him. Last month, Rakesh and Arati had taken him to Singapore and so he had missed the monthly visit. And she herself had been too busy rushing around, making ends meet, to really miss him deeply.

Do I even miss him as much as I should? Often her self-doubt surfaced, leaving her highly disturbed. How much were you supposed to miss a child who had been separated from you for over three years? He was now 11, and would be legally an adult by the time she found her financial feet (it was really taking long) and asked for custody. And Rakesh was so stupid about this son thing. 'I will look after my son, you only have to look after yourself', he had said, kindly.

Wonder why they don't have any children of their own—I wonder if Arati can have kids, she thought, unemotional about her ex-husband and his current wife.

But Babloo will be here, she thought with pleasure and planned a few goodies for him. She would take him to McDonald's, or should she cook the chole-bhature that he had always loved as child? Well, they could do both. One on Saturday evening, the other on Sunday morning. She had already sent her invoice to her online, unseen employers and the wire transfer for her commercial writing would be in soon. She could then cheerfully offer her son a double scoop of Baskin-Robbins, and maybe new clothes for Diwali—or that could wait until the next month.

I'll tackle two more vocabulary sheets and get that story done, so I am free the weekend.

* *

Jerry's Story

For days after the incident, I would walk along the beach talking to the fishermen, asking them if they remembered Natasha. Foreigners were often friendly and people remembered them. Yes, they had seen her around, more frequently since the rains had abated, with the gang of young Russian people. They did the usual things—played in the water, sunbathed, read huge tomes—but not many of them went parasailing or anything like that.

The shops in the main street remembered her much better. The library cum bookshop cum knick-knacks shop owner said she was a kind soul who once lent her money. Not a huge amount—about Rs. 2,000. The wine store guy said she regularly bought vodka and sometimes wine.

Did she drink all that much? Did Maria get a lot of vodka bottles in the trash? I must ask her.

I wasn't sure where my train of thought was taking me. *What am I going to discover?*

I went up and searched her room, although it had been picked clean by the police. Maybe I was looking for hidden letters, some hidden clue that would throw light on why she had been the victim. Had she overdosed herself? Then why was she naked? Had that boy been there with her, had they 'been together', then he had forced her to take an overdose?

She must have died instantly. He got scared, ran back to this resort and the whole gang must have checked out immediately and disappeared.

'Bad news from home' is what they had told the reception, when asked for the reason for their hasty departure.

This was where the vortex ended. I went back to where I had started. The beach, the shops . . . no clue, no solution.

Maria and I went to church. As always, the old stone walls and their musty smell gave huge amounts of comfort. I went into confession. I spoke of fear, the fear of death, fear of uncertainty, fear of not knowing what had happened there, fear that someday it would all boomerang, and we innocent victims would be caught in a web not of our making. All we wanted was a peaceful life. What had we done to bother anyone? Why did we have to face this? I also said that we did not deserve the ghost stories that had stopped guests from visiting our homestay. Our only means of livelihood was being taken away from us. Whatever were we to do?

The pastor told me to have courage. That God had a plan. No one would really suffer if they listened to God's voice, to their own inner voice. And if we did suffer, meaning we did face trials and tribulations, we should know that perhaps we had erred somewhere, sometime, and were receiving our just desserts. We had something to learn that would help us reach him. The Lord was merciful. Once he was sure that we were repentant, good things would happen again, we would forever remain in his warm embrace.

I was not really convinced by what seemed like a simplistic, fatalistic explanation.

Whatever will be, will be. Grin and bear it. And then it would become all right.

Of course it would become all right, if we grinned and bore it. I thanked Father and we left the church, feeling somewhat incomplete.

Jerry reread his writing. He realized that there was very little about Natasha and more about himself and Maria. But what could he have written about Natasha? They knew precious little about the case.

* *

Kayuru

By Johny Kutty

It was Sunday, calm and serene. No one was about. Except Surya. He owned the place and could be there any time he wanted to. He liked to think of himself as a kind and just employer—even though he imposed his own laws on work and pay. But he felt he was justified in that. After all, he had built his business from scratch, working 16 hours a day when he had no one. Now that he had grown to one of the largest producers of coir products, he had a right to enjoy his fiefdom.

* *

He was struggling, his legs jerking with the effort to breathe against the strong coir rope pressed again this neck. He was proud of the coir from his factory, it was one of the best. It took a decade of sun and rain to reduce it to dust. His eyes goggled in his face, red and watery. Sweat first beaded and then streamed off his chocolate-brown skin. He half-sat, half-lay in the dusty yard, the soft mud forming slush on his body. He raised his arms to his throat, tried to loosen the rope. A sharp tug reminded him that he was not alone.

Work-roughened hands tugged; he knew he was overpowered. The clink of the bangles increased his shame. Ten minutes ago he had slid his thumb beneath the ring of glass bangles and caressed the owner's inner wrist suggestively. She had responded by putting her arms around his neck; his own hands went down to caress the rounded hips. She had worn the sari vampishly low, a length of coir rope around her waist. Surya had untied it and tugged her closer to him. He hardly knew when Kanaka took it from him, writhing against him. There was promise in her eyes as she pressed into him. She playfully closed his eyes, then went behind him and threw the rope across his chest. In a trice, she kicked her knee against the back of his. He buckled and the rope slid upward, choking him. She twisted and tightened it cunningly at the nape of his neck; it was her tool of trade and she knew it well.

Not bad, thought Rambler. *Maybe I should make Kanaka more seductive.* His story was going to be about a coir producer who makes inappropriate advances to the minor daughter of one of his workers, a woman, and tries to pay her hush money. The mother, Kanaka, threatens to take matters to the trade union, but these were the days before the Coir Act of 1953 was enforced and she could not make her voice heard. Rambler had decided to make Surya so drunk on his fistful of power that he offers the widow sexual favours, although obliquely. Now really enraged, Kanaka takes him up on that. She catches him alone at his house on Sunday, and decides to kill him. What actually happens is told only at the end of the story.

Rambler could not resist riding his hobby horse—the Coir Board and its history. It was partly to do with Shiny, he knew. Anyway, back to the story. He was fascinated by the precise terminology of the coir

175

business. Coir fibre meant the extract of the husk, coir husk meant tied and untied husk, coir yarn meant spun fibre, and so on. He intended to trace the process of manufacture in his story as well as trace the history of the coir business from its early days till the time the co-operatives were formed. There was plenty of written material for him to browse and a multitude of pictures to help him describe people and places, which was his métier.

* *

'Ruchi ke liye rishte aaye hain', Namrata informed her brother and husband at dinner that day that Ruchi was beginning to receive marriage proposals.

'Naturally', said Nikhil, not very interested.

'She's meeting them on Sunday', Namrata further volunteered, to no one in particular.

Silence fell as they all got engrossed in the TV serial.

Rajesh took a postprandial stroll in the compound. He was leaving the next day.

At 8 a.m., Mr. Sharma was surprised to see a strange man standing at his door asking for Ruchi.

'Rohan Mehra?' He said the first thing that came to his head.

'No, sir. Rajesh Vashisht. I am Namrata's brother.'

Mr. Sharma continued to look perplexed, but invited him in. Ruchi came out, looked surprised to see him. Quickly, she made the introductions and explanations.

'I am leaving for Nanded today. And I came to make a job offer to Ruchi, in case she is interested.'

He briefed them on Nanak Institute and what they did.

'Ah . . . you want her to go to Nanded?'

'Yes, well—'

'No, no, Ruchi intends to marry soon', said Mrs. Sharma firmly.

'*Shaadi kar ke le jaaun toh*?' (Suppose I take her as my wife?)

The Sharma family gawked, speechless.

'Look, I have to go now. But I will come back next week. Think about it, we will talk then.' Rajesh was looking at Mr. Sharma, but actually talking to Ruchi.

Ruchi's heart thudded. It was the suddenness of the whole thing, she told herself.

Her parents looked at her. 'Ma, Papa . . . I don't know why he came. I did not ask him to come over here. I have not even thought about him in that way.'

'Has he said anything to Namrata? Did Namrata say anything to you?'

'No . . . I mean, I don't know what he said to Namrata, but Namrata said nothing to me.'

'Do you like him, Ruchi?'

'Ma, I have spoken to him only once. And I just told you, I don't think of him like that.'

'So you don't want to marry him?' asked her father.

'Papa, I don't know . . . I don't know if he is my type.'

'*Yeh type kya hota hai*?' Her mother was dismissive. Marriage fixing was serious business and she had no time for trivialities like 'type'.

'Ruchi, would you like to marry him?' Mr. Sharma interrupted his wife.

'Papa, I don't *know*.'

'OK, OK, beta . . . calm down. You have time to decide. He is coming back in a week. Think about it. Your mother and I will find out more about the family from Nikhil. In the meantime, you can meet the photograph boy on Sunday. Then you can marry who you like. Meet both the boys in the photo, if you like.'

Mr Sharma was calm and practical. Rajeev, her brother, was only beginning to show a glimmer of interest. Of course, he would miss her and all that, but he would have the living room to himself at night, and that was 'nothing to be sneezed at'; he grinned as he remembered Father Joseph's favourite phrase.

Mrs Sharma was excited and energized. Two approvals and one direct proposal for her daughter! That was luscious fare to serve to the ladies of the building, especially the Rajesh chapter. There was precious little romance in these tiny one-bedroom apartments. To fall in love amidst the grime and heat of Mumbai and its depressing little spaces called for jubilation.

Ruchi would make the right choice, of that she had no doubt. Women were canny creatures, and her primordial female instinct would help her make a wise decision. She would go for the man who most made her feel settled and secure.

That afternoon, when Ruchi went upstairs, Namrata was all glowing and smiles.

'Ruchiiii,' she teased. That afternoon, Namrata ran her through a multitude of pictures on her mobile phone—photographs of her home in Nanded, Rajesh's new Honda Jazz, the gurdwara, her simple parents. She smiled at Ruchi's awkwardness—'I know, nothing is decided yet, Ruchi. Don't worry. I just want you to know that if you marry Rajesh, you will be in comfortable surroundings. And I think he really has fallen in love with you. My goodness, I can hardly believe it!'

'But you go and meet those other boys. These things have to be done. Uncle and Auntie have said you must meet them, so you must. And don't worry. We will remain friends.' Her words were reassuring, but her attitude was the slightly proprietorial one that is reserved for one's relatives.

Ruchi was suddenly thankful that she had not confided a great deal about Sanjay. She messaged him to meet her that Saturday. They met and in no uncertain terms she told him that they could not meet anymore. She was a little piqued that he appeared quite unconcerned and even relieved. Well, that was one thing taken care of. That night she sat for a long time, with her pen and paper. She thought of Dilip Kumar and wrote nothing.

Rohan Mehra came around on Sunday morning to take her out. He was tall and nice-looking; a little young, she felt. They went to Inorbit Mall. It was really noisy.

'Isn't there somewhere quieter?' he enquired.

Well, there's Four Seasons, but it's really expensive. Ruchi did not voice this thought and suggested a smaller place nearby. It was noisy too, but there was a family room. Rohan saw KFC and they headed there. It was too hot and stuffy to eat and Ruchi only picked at the bucket of chicken he had ordered. They chatted over chicken and Coke, chatted about this and that. People found it easy to talk to Ruchi, and Rohan was telling her about his job at the software firm, his work hours and salary. If he was disappointed at her lack of reaction to his delicious six-figure salary, he did not show it. They parted amicably.

Rajesh arrived on Wednesday, ostensibly for a professional reason. Namrata shooed the two of them away and they went to the faithful Inorbit. It was far quieter today. Their low voices seemed to echo in the near empty food court.

'Ruchi, I am sure I took you by surprise. Believe me, I surprised myself', began Rajesh after an awkward pause. 'I like you a lot. I am normally very shy.'

He hoped she would say something. She didn't. He continued.

'Nanded is a small town. We are one of the prestigious families there. The institute is my dream. And I need a partner who is intelligent and shares my dream. You are so bubbly and you get along so well with people. It would help me. And,' he added confidently, 'I am sure you will enjoy the challenge as well.'

'So it's an arranged marriage?' Ruchi was half defiant, half disappointed. She did so want to be passionately in love.

'I like you, Ruchi!' Rajesh pointed out. 'I am ready to marry and I think you are the person for me,' he burst out. 'Unless there is someone you already like . . . Namrata said that you were meeting some guys your parents had selected.'

'No . . . but . . .' Ruchi trailed off.

They ate. Ruchi took a deep breath and told him about Sanjay. She went red as she told him that they had gone to second base. At his perplexed expression, her courage almost failed her. She steeled herself to say, 'We were quite physical . . . with each other . . .'

Rajesh said nothing, Ruchi neither. They started moving out. Ruchi did not blame him for rejecting a fast Mumbai girl. Rajesh suddenly pulled her to an empty table and sat her on the chair. 'I also had a girlfriend, loved her deeply. But Nanded is a small town. And naturally we did not go to any base. I did not think to tell you because that was a long time ago. It doesn't matter now. I would remain totally committed to you. And that is what I expect from my wife, Ruchi.'

This simple young man in his unfashionable gray shirt and terry-cotton trousers was looking at the fashionable young miss from Mumbai with warm, sincere eyes and Ruchi knew at that instant that she belonged with him.

* *

Monica sat back in the comfortable Honda City, not fretting. Since the epistolary romance, both fictional and real, she had begun to feel good about almost everything. Take now, for instance: they were stuck in a traffic jam at Ambedkar Nagar. Normally she would feel impatient, or tap away on her mobile phone. She would have sent Anil a message that she was getting delayed, as if it was somehow his fault. Now she just looked around her. She watched as the driver rolled down his window and sought the blessing of a begging eunuch. The street kids were swarming around with little national flags, gleaming strawberries in little boxes, or little plastic toys that would not survive more than ten minutes with any four-year-old. The eyes of some of the older children were white and expressionless and made Monica shiver. From time to time, they would pull out a dirty rag from the pocket of their grubby shorts and sniff at it.

'What are they smelling, Ramakant? These little children?'

'Shoe polish or something they put on their *roomal* and smell, madam.' Ramakant was a graduate and proud of his English-speaking skills. 'Then they don't feel hungry.' Monica felt a jolt. She was so out of touch with Mumbai, where she had spent nearly two decades. *My prize money is definitely going for street children*, she decided.

But first she had to get that story written. She was not getting any further with the letter-story. Ideas were not flowing thick and fast as she had hoped they would. Maybe today would yield something. She was on her way to a meeting of the Lit Club. A Geeta Iyengar of Indus Books had been invited. She was a neighbour of Janaki's, where she was now headed. Janaki lived in a newly developed property in Dadar and it was a long drive.

Janaki's housing society was practically a replica of her own Cuffe Parade colony. Landscaped gardens, swimming pool and tennis courts, large gleaming cars parked neatly in the stilt parking—the works. There was hardly a soul to be seen, the tennis courts were bereft of players and the pool looked formidable. Monica did not see herself swimming in a pool, watched by unknown eyes from the buildings surrounding it. It was creepy. Was her place creepy to others?

Janaki had made typical South Indian fare, which they were to have after Geeta spoke about the short story competition. Geeta did not say much, except exhorting them to write—'There is still time.' She did not mention that she would be one of the editors. They spoke a little about how short stories needed to come to the point very quickly, nothing else. Janaki brought out her cocktail idlis and delicious coconut chutney. Washed down by genuine filter coffee, it was a highly satisfying repast. Monica sauntered over to the balcony.

'Akash Raj and Piah', said Janaki's voice behind her, pointing vaguely to one of the middle floors in the building opposite. She looked pleased, as if living in the proximity of two film stars was something she deserved credit for. 'I think they are splitting, though. He is hardly there, most of the time.' Monica got goosebumps seeing the deserted outdoors. The only people about seemed the maids and the dog walkers and the drivers happily waiting under the shade of a sculpted tree. *Do people even talk to each other anymore?*

Monica skipped dinner that night. Anil was out for a corporate dinner and the children were studying. Or the children were in their rooms, to be precise. They were regular kids; she did not think they had any major problems. She was sure that they all loved each other, although no one was particularly demonstrative. She knocked on her daughter's door—'What's up, Mini?'

'Hey, Ma. Nothing, Ma, just catching up with friends.' Her son was actually working on his maths. She felt reassured but a little alone. When they were younger, they would chat each day after school. She had attended all their school functions, stage plays, and matches, been more and more with them as Anil had gotten busier and busier and they had drifted apart. *Well, that's taken care of now,* she thought, smiling.

When Anil got back, they chatted a little, cuddled a little, and slept. Anil slept; he was tired and the three large whiskeys sped him along to dreamland. Monica lay awake, listening to the owls. Toss and turn. Toss and turn. She got up for a cup of tea. Went onto the balcony and looked at the city that never slept. LED lamps glowed gently along the common roads that ran through their spacious gated community. It was darkness in most of the buildings; only a few lighted squares shone. She looked beyond the boundary walls from her tenth-floor flat. It was reassuring to see a few old trees casting large uneven shadows on the otherwise bright street. There was a car or two at 3.30 a.m. A startled bird flapped out of nowhere and disappeared into the darkness. 'Tu-whoo, tu-whoo.' The owl on the chajja stared back at her when she followed its sound and located it.

Can one be at peace and, within that peace, also a little restless? Bits and pieces of her life flashed through her head. Her focus as a schoolgirl—she used to be a sought-after actress for the annual drama competition. From an all-girls' school to a co-educational college— she had fallen in love with at least five people in her three years at college and had shocked herself by doing so. However, she had dated only Mohit and then he went off to join the IMA and they lost touch. Then she had married Anil. Amidst living the good life, they had to deal with the death of two out of four parents, a few family and social crises—and here they were, a little bruised and battered by life, but still going. In her hitherto goalless life, she had found a small goal, the story! And the prize money for street children! She fully intended to work at it. After that . . . she would think of that later.

The babble of the evening's Lit Club meeting began crowding her mind; an idea emerged and slowly formed.

* *

Vikram had stepped out for a walk, glad to escape. For some reason today, he decided to visit the Tapkeshwar temple. It was a 4-kilometre round trip. Normally he took a 2-kilometre walk, so he decided to take an autorickshaw to the temple and walk back. He could not remember when he had last visited a temple. Probably with Reema. Maybe he would sit there for a while—that would be enough time for the hullabaloo at home to die out. Bhabhiji had invited her friends for *satsang*. She had graciously asked '*devarji*' to stay, but he pleaded a walk as being essential for his health. The idea of meeting with garrulous women of various shapes and sizes did not appeal to him.

Tapkeshwar was quite busy at this time of the evening. It was even busier on Mondays. Garhwalis are a devout lot. Mountain dwellers often are—they live so close to nature and its hazards, they respect that and also respect everything that they believe will protect them. He chose a spot and sat quietly for a while. He thought a little of Reema and Abhay. He was not reflecting, nor praying. His mind fell quiet. He was in a state of no thought. It was bliss. He walked back joyously, almost buoyantly and arrived earlier than he had hoped.

The second-last bhajan, dedicated to Santoshi Ma and sung to the tune of the popular Hindi song 'pardesiya, yeh sach hai piya' was being belted out at top volume by an energetic old lady. He would have slipped into his study, but *bhabhiji* motioned for him to join them for the final Om Jai Jagadish. Half-in, half-out, Vikram stood at the door and let his heart sway to the soulful melody.

The pious ladies then devoted their energies to consuming the delicious chole and hot bhature that Bhado was bringing in. Vikram excused himself now and freshened up. When he came out, the ladies had left and he settled into his favourite chair while Bhado fetched his whiskey. Bhabhiji came along and regaled him with the latest gossip. Mrs Nautiyal's daughter had been selected for a job abroad, Louisiana, USA. They were desperate to get her engaged before she left. They did not want her marrying some 'Amreekan'. Mrs Bahuguna's son had earned a promotion, he was now brigadier. Mrs Somebody's somebody did something . . . Vikram listened with half an ear.

Bhabhiji then spoke of Reema and Abhay. There was a subdued silence. '*Bhado bhi toh apna bachcha hai.*' Vikram asserted that Bhado was also like his son and promptly summoned him. He enquired about his birth certificate. There was bound to be some useful document in the caboodle that his parents had kept stashed in a suitcase under their bed or someplace else. They needed Bhado's birth certificate to initiate any proceedings for his recruitment into the army. If his parents did not have the birth certificate, they would have to search through the records of the Dehradun Nagar Nigam, which kept all the records of births and deaths of Mussoorie and Dehradun.

Meanwhile, Bhado had smartened up considerably. Buaji had taught him how to cook many types of food. An army wife herself, she had picked up Chinese and continental dishes, in addition to the now pan-Indian idlis and dosas. Bhado had great fun learning, even greater fun buying the ingredients at the smart stores near the clock tower. He was now an accomplished cook. And Vikram enjoyed the delicate fried chicken, soup, and bread that he served him for dinner, instead of the oily bhatura and spicy chole. Tired and happy, Vikram slept soundly. He never woke up.

He was stiff and cold when Bhado went to wake him up at 4 a.m. He woke buaji and they both stared in despair at each other for a long time. The clock struck five. They started calling people. It was Bhado who called Raghav, Sekhon, and the rest of the bridge crowd. The cremation took place the same day, and Raghav returned with buaji and Bhado to Vikram's residence. He stayed the night. The next morning, he went through Vikram's papers, mainly searching for the memoirs. He was determined to get them into some shape and see their accession to a library, probably at the Military Academy. Sekhon had offered to take over that aspect, if Raghav got the papers in shape.

* *

Lalima

Vineet was a poor little rich boy and Lalima was a poor little poor girl. She wasn't really poor—just not-so-rich. Her mother taught at the swank school, Greenwich International—which is why she got a fee waiver and could study there. Vineet was her classmate and they were both 9 years old.

They had to together produce an English project on a writer of their choice. The cerebral Vineet had no idea because the only things he read were the instructions to his computer games. The dreamy Lalima had wanted Enid Blyton. No one ever read Enid Blyton anymore. Unfortunately, they did not feature on the list given by Rakshita Ma'am, their English teacher.

Lalima chose Roald Dahl over Ruskin Bond from the list and Vineet just went along with that. Each team was expected to do the following:

- Write a short biography of the author.

- List ten new words from his stories and write their meanings, use them in sentences.

- Write a story that they felt their author should write.

'Vineet, I am not going to do everything', Lalima had warned. So Vineet had worked and their initial research revealed Dahl's Norwegian origins.

This story is really not going anywhere, thought Maya. Even the twenty thousand rupees looked remote; two lakhs were light years away. *Think, Maya, think.*

Maya began again—another story about a girl called Lalima. Why Lalima? She had no clue. She just loved the positive feel the word gave her.

Lalima

Lalima jumped excitedly up and down in her humble tin-roofed abode. Her father, Prakash Yadav, looked indulgently at his little Chutki, whom they now formally called Lalima. Or to put it precisely, that was the name his wife's memsahib had given her. Sheela worked as a maidservant in the tall buildings, across the road from where they stayed. She was not back home yet to witness her daughter's unbridled glee.

The reason for the joy was Lalima's admission to the Greenwich International School, under RTE, the Right to Education Act. RTE made it incumbent upon private non-minority schools, such as Greenwich, to reserve at least 25 per cent of their seats for children from the poorer economic sections. There was an entrance test that the children had to pass. Sheela and Prakash were grateful that the employer had turned benefactor, coached their bright little girl, and helped secure her admission to a good school. This was the beginning of their troubles.

Prakash was a gardener at Greenwich. On day 1, he held the excited Lalima's hand and deposited her outside class 4C. Wide-eyed, well-dressed children eyed each other warily. Some others did not— they had probably been together at Greenwich Kindergarten. Lalima belonged to neither group. No one else had a parent with a menial job at their school.

* *

'Your papa is a bhaiya, your papa is a bhaiya'—Lalima had been in tears each night in her one month at school. Her crime was that she was the gardener bhaiya's daughter.

Their neighbor, Anjali the fruit seller, had come in to advise. 'Why didn't you put her in another school?' she asked, wondering how such a common-sense thing could have escaped the ambitious parents. She went on to embroider a tale about 'those children from the big houses'.

* *

Maya planned to have a fairy or a benevolent god appear in Lalima's dreams and help her cope, also help her see the dignity of her father's labour. There would be instances when Lalima would refuse to enter the school with Prakash; he would be hurt but would not show it. There could be another girl or boy, from an older class, who was also from her shanty and how he helps her cope.

Maya made herself a cup of tea and chewed on her ideas. It had better be good. Not just good—spectacular! And with good dialogues. She began noting down the snippets of conversation that she heard on her walk to and from college. Rendering them with just the right mix of Hindi and English would be the challenge. She could not afford to lose readers who did not relate to Hindi. There was a lot of modelling to be done.

* *

The repairs and renovation were progressing. The cafe had always been a cheerful little place; now that part of it had been destroyed, they decided to redo it stylishly. Maria was completely taken by the kitchens she saw on TV. She had now become a faithful viewer of Nigella and *Rachel Allen: Bake!* Those large ovens, the central island—their little space simply would not accommodate all of that. They could not go up—have another makeshift storey—there was no place. They had to expand the space, within the existing space. They had seen how these *kirana* shop owners (the Marwari grocers) lived—families, and generations of families, grew and flourished in that mezzanine above the ground-floor shop. It was illegal, but no one did anything about it. They were always very quiet. When their children spilled outside to play, the father, the shopkeeper, replied, tongue in cheek, 'Oh, they have just come to meet me. My family lives down the road in a kholi' (a little room). Jerry and Maria were amused that even their fibs were of a modest scale. They could at least lie that they lived in a two-bedroom flat in the village!

The bottom line was that space could be created. They had to start the remodelling soon. The single oven and the three-burner gas stove were proving a little inadequate. At least another oven was needed.

Then Maria had an idea. Suppose they did build a mezzanine? And moved the entire seating up there? They had very young customers, who would not mind climbing stairs.

'And we can have low-rising steps. Let's check out designs.'

There was a library down the road, and they had created a lovely children's section in the mezzanine. The proprietor, a lady, assured her that children were comfortable, reading their books for hours. Her rule was 'You have to remove your footwear to go up. It makes cleaning that much easier.' Maria was sure she could explore options. Armed with many *Indoor Outdoor* magazines amongst the other foreign glossies, Maria returned and the two of them pored over the designs. They all were way beyond their budget.

After a good deal of research and consultation from friends and well-wishers, and some serious number crunching, they decided on an open kitchen plan. The ceiling would have to be a little low, so that the mezzanine on top could have adequate headroom. Powerful chimneys were their answer to odours and fumes. There was also the matter of funnelling out the fumes towards the sky, outside; if they did not do as specified by the corporation, their shop license was in danger. They opted for charcoal filter models; the recurrent cost of changing the filter each month was preferred over ugly tubes traversing the length of the kitchen and out and the sky-funnel, as they had privately termed it. The shop license was safe too. Moreover, Maria's food was generally baked and that did not create a lot of fumes.

The Souzas had to shut shop for a month, there was no option. They had been lucky to find local carpenters, fabricators, and electricians to do the work. These guys were experienced, and had apprentices who had trained under them for years, so if the master was not available, the disciple was. Jerry and Maria tried to run a tight ship, but there were delays. There was absenteeism, especially with the carpenter. He had an ad hoc force that disappeared if there was a festival or a wedding or a death. It was an ad hoc business. Look what had happened to the Assamese boys employed by restaurateurs. They had all returned home in droves following a disturbance in Assam and its fallout in other parts of the country, leaving their employers high and dry.

But the Souzas were luckier than the hapless restaurant owners. The fabricators and the electricians completed on schedule. Through one of their young customers, they met a decorator who designed an unconventional mezzanine. It was essentially a slowly rising staircase, each step a large square, enough for a table for two. There were four such levels. The stairs led to the mezzanine, which effectively covered the kitchen below. The mezzanine would accommodate four or five tables, each seating four.

The sturdy, gleaming wooden staircase began assuming shape and the Souzas started feeling that their little cafe was coming back to them. Jerry turned his attention to his story again. Natasha! The story had to be more about her!

They were to go to Goa to order some furniture for the shop. They knew where to get it cheap, and they would charge only a reasonable amount for shipping it to their doorstep in Pune.

They would also visit their homestay in Colva.

* *

Jerry and Maria took the Goa Express from Pune to Madgaon. They would pick up their furniture from some of the local shops. Goans were fond of their furniture. Good wooden furniture, stylishly antique was their preference. Cane was also popular. This would be available in the smaller shops in nondescript side streets. Some manufacturers, like the Kings Cane Craft had made a name for themselves. But a number of small artisans worked marvellous rattan pieces and enjoyed word-of-mouth reputation.

The Souzas put up at Aunt Nellie's. She was a distant aunt and welcomed them to her homestay; otherwise, most homestays welcomed foreigners more than Indians. In two days, they had selected their chairs, tables, sideboards, the last especially made to order for their tiny space. The open shelves had been done by the carpenter in Pune.

'Jerry, let's buy this pot holder, or maybe two of them. And I really liked these lampshades! See these ones. They will go with the decor.'

'We will pack nicely and give, madam. No breaking.'

'Can you deliver everything to our shop in Pune?'

It was early September, and raining hard in Goa. Both work and transport were delayed on this account.

'If no rain, then we can give in two weeks. Transport will depend on rain. If it rains very much, truck will go slowly.'

Happy with their purchases, the Souzas returned to Aunt Nellie's, gave her a huge hug and two-thousand-rupee notes that brought a beaming smile to her plump face. They set off for Colva, hearts beating fast. They went and stood outside the erstwhile Souza's Homestay; it was now simply called The Resort.

They watched as a woman, laden with a large stuffed bag made her way to the gate. She rang the doorbell and Annie, their Annie, came out to answer. The Souzas went in as well.

'Oh, madam, you have come back!'

'How is everything, Annie?'

'It is good, madam. One minute, madam.'

She turned to deal with the other lady, obviously a foreigner, probably Russian. Something about her reminded Maria about Natasha.

'This . . . Souza Homestay?'

Maria, Annie, and Jerry looked at each other.

Jerry stepped forward.

'I am Jerry Souza and this is my wife, Maria. We used to run Souza Homestay.'

'And you are?' asked Maria, her heart beating very fast.

'Viktoriya . . . Viktoriya Krasnov.' Natasha Krasnov's mother held out her hand.

Natasha's mother did not speak very fluent English. Annie, by now, had picked up some Russian, so between the four of them, they managed.

'I get . . . ash, *da*', she said, holding up her cupped palms.

'Annie, are Natasha's things still in the garage?' Maria asked. There was room at The Resort, so all three of them could be accommodated.

Maria and Viktoriya went down to the garage. Most of the things were musty and damp. Viktoriya wept as she picked out a locket, which contained a picture of Natasha and an old boyfriend. She had not known that her daughter still held him so close to her heart. She looked at the many books and clothes. They were in a state of decay. There was one good sweater, though. She did not like to give a murdered woman's sweater to anyone, so she simply squared her shoulders and breathed deeply.

'We burn . . .' She pronounced it 'bairn' and rolled the r.

With the owner's permission, the four of them carried everything to the corner of the backyard and watched the flames consume it. It took a while and smoked a lot, but eventually it was done.

That evening they all went for a walk along the beach. Viktoriya spoke a lot. A lot of that was in Russian and the Souzas could vaguely gather that she had lost her husband, soon after she heard about Natasha. He had a weak heart and she had not told him that they had lost her. Nevertheless, he had died. She had come down to see her daughter's final resting place.

'You want to track the case. Pin down the offender.'

'*Da?*' Jerry spoke more slowly, in simple English and she appeared to comprehend. 'I go back', she said decisively. 'Natasha, here.' She indicated her bosom.

'Doesn't she want to know who murdered her daughter?' a surprised Maria asked later.

'It could take years. How much time can she spend alone in a strange country? Better go back and pray for the soul, Natasha's and the murderer's.'

'Hmm . . .' Maria slept. Jerry didn't. That night he stayed awake and wrote out his story.

* *

Closure

By Jerry Souza

They were at the chapel. They prayed, all three of them—father, mother, and son—Samuel, Esther, and Luke Fernandes. They prayed for old Thomas, Samuel's father. He had disappeared, this very day. Three years ago.

Samuel was a professor of humanities at the Modern Engineering College, Majali, Goa. These days they taught the humanities at technical colleges—holistic education and all that! The college was very recently established, and Marine Structures was the core discipline. They lived on the campus, which was just a half kilometre from the Arabian Sea. It was a small and cosy community.

The Fernandeses lived in a well appointed house; it was an apartment—one of a block of four—on the ground floor. Esther happily tended the tiny garden and was also computer operator at the office. Luke attended primary school on the campus. In a few years, they would have to think of moving away so Luke could attend a larger and better school. But for now, they were happy. Thomas used to enjoy his walks, and get back a small gift for his grandson each day.

One day he bought a small plastic car. Only it wasn't what Luke wanted.

'I like that big red car, Ajja.'

'I will get for you, tomorrow, boy.'

'No, today, Ajja, I want it today.'

'Luke, enough. Ignore him, Pappa.' Esther called out from the garden.

'It's not far . . .' The old man muttered as he went to return the toy.

That was the last they saw of him. Had he stepped out of the campus? People knew them. Someone would have told them. They searched homes of friends and relatives, then every home on the campus. They searched the hospital, and a week later, even the morgue. Nothing. Samuel hired two divers with almost a sense of futility. They came up with nothing.

The uneasy agitation became part of their existence. Luke cried every evening for several months. 'Where is Ajja?' he would ask a hundred times. He never played with a car again.

* *

They were subdued, as they always were, when they left the chapel.

'Please, Pappa, guide us to you. Dear God, guide us to him.' Samuel prayed for the millionth time.

Jerry's story showed how the family was living out each day, weighed by guilt.

Two more years passed. Luke would soon need a better school. Samuel applied for jobs in the bigger Goan cities; he had even been accepted by some. But he backed out each time. *What if Pappa comes here and finds we are gone?'*

Esther saw the familiar white rectangle on Samuel's desk. She turned it over. Goa University. 'This is as good as it can get, but how can we desert Pappa?'

They did not speak about it at all. Life carried on. They went to church on Sunday, still very quiet. If Samuel did not accept the job by Monday, it would go. No one slept very well that night.

Luke was the first to speak next morning. 'Mama, Pappa, Ajja came in my dream yesterday.'

'What did he say?'

'He said, *Take heart, son, your sins are forgiven.'*

'Ajja forgives me, Ajja forgives me!' Luke was dancing all around the room. Luke was now old enough to understand that if he had not insisted on the car that evening, his grandfather might still be here. He had been six then, and no one blamed him for it. But as he grew older, he had begun to feel that perhaps he had been responsible for his grandfather's disappearance.

'Esther', Samuel began hesitantly. 'You know, Esther, I saw Pappa, too. Two nights ago. He said, *I have fought the good fight, I have finished the race, I have kept the faith.*'

'What?' he asked, at Esther's incredulous look.

'Sam, Pappa told me, in my dream, yesterday, *We live by faith, not by sight.*'

* *

The story, naturally, ended on a happy note with the family taking the decision to move to Goa University. The family still did not know for certain what had happened to Thomas, but now they were reconciled with that uncertainty. Jerry had wanted to convey this and he was not sure if he had successfully done that.

* *

The mails had been pouring in thick and fast. The inboxes of the four editors bulged with their share of material to be edited. Meher was apportioning them randomly. They would first long list the entries, and after a three-step editing process, arrive at the shortlist.

The stories that made it to the long list would have to be error-free. Of course, minor typos would be ignored, but major and consistent grammatical glitches would send the piece double-quick into the recycle bin. It was amazing how many of these they received.

'Lots of wannabes out there', Ramona always used to say. And if publishing houses rejected them, they smartly went online and self-published. They would go in for e-books and, sometimes, print versions. POD—print on demand, it was called. 'Vanity publishing' was the derisive term the professional publishers used for these guys. To be fair, self-publishing also had its formats and norms, and the publishers did offer their editorial and proofreading services to those who wanted them. After all, even the self-publishing portals had to develop and build their own reputations. They were, very slowly, gathering a reputation in India. But by and large, it was a traditional publishing world, with tremendous amounts of prestige and romance associated with paper books, published by known houses.

By September 22, Vidya, Melvin, Geeta, and Usha were ploughing through a mountain of stories. These had passed the first screening—grammar, and of course, timely submission. Not a single late entry was entertained. Often, it would happen that a truly brilliant and creative mind would churn out a really superb tale— but the command of the English language was wanting. Or he would simply turn it in late, as was the habit of geniuses. 'Too bad' was Ramona's verbal directive. Indus simply did not have the time to go through mounds of rubbishy grammar for a little glimmer of gold dust. As for the possible hidden gem among the late entries—that was simply a chance they would have to take.

Stage 1 consisted of shortlisting ten stories each. This, the four editors would do independently. In the next stage, each of the forty stories would be circulated and ranked, by each of the editors. These would be compiled by Meher, in readiness for stage 3. Ramona would also read them, but she was sort of outside the working committee. Her job was to troubleshoot, serve her opinions and assessments as tiebreaker, soothe nerves and calm tempers. Everyone was overworked. Innumerable coffees, and also dinner and dessert were all on the house, and a ride home when needed. These guys had to practically live at the office. A lot was at stake.

'I could, you know, not bathe nor shave, and just live at the office in these very clothes' was Melvin's generous offer, obviously refused by his colleagues.

Vidya was cranky at having to stop the children's literature work and do this. 'If any of these stories turns out to be good children's fiction, we will use it' was Ram Mohan's platitude.

Usha and Geeta worked steadily on, each trying to outdo the other in speed and in the unnecessarily lyrical comments they posted on the Excel sheet given by Meher for their ten stories. For a week, they had worked around the clock. Then they all took a short holiday after stage 1—which meant that they left early and arrived late the next day!

Stage 2

Forty stories! They had to read the thirty stories sent in by the others and comment on them as well. In addition, they had to read their own ten stories again, if they felt it was warranted, and modify the comments that they had posted on the Excel sheets. Rank them too, from 1 to 40. This last part took longer than anything else. They ranked and re-ranked, then forgot why one story had got fifth rank and the other tenth rank. Melvin had a great memory and good mental organization—the forty stories were already good friends, living in different addresses of his brain. He did not have to reread, as the stressed-out Vidya had to. She changed her rankings at least five times before making them final.

Usha and Geeta were focused and systematic, zealous warriors. Usha even had her own personal colour-coded spreadsheet for each of the forty stories, which she planned to share only in the final stage. She meant to subtly point out to Ramona that *her* spreadsheet was lacking some parameters for assessment. She would hand it out to the others in that meeting.

Geeta did what was required of her and passed pointedly by Usha's workstation several times a day.

One more 24/7 week and the 40-story Excel sheet was ready. Meher worked on a few formulae, compiled them story-wise, averaged out the rankings and they were ready with the shortlist.

Stage 3

Discussions began the very next day. Ramona and Ram Mohan, who had both read the stories, were also present. Ten stories that consistently drew the lowest ten rankings were eliminated, at the outset.

'This is not a very efficient way to do it', Usha insisted, as she handed out her spreadsheets. 'See, I have included categories in each genre. Each story is different, unique and Indus must publish only the best.'

'You are right, Usha.' Ram Mohan was not unaware of Usha's desire to upstage Ramona, Geeta, or whoever else she could. 'But this time we will work with broader parameters, we have been a little rushed and disorganized. Let's just go with our spreadsheet, shall we? It's already the fifth of October!'

They worked hard to cull twelve stories for their anthology. Heads were pounding, eyes were smarting and ears buzzing, and the conference room began smelling of used coffee cups and Melvin's cigarette smoke.

'This is the Love Me, Love My Ciggies Week, guys.'

He was ungentlemanly enough to ignore Vidya's delicate sniffing.

Ramona and Ram Mohan burned their lungs in the smoking area, as befitted their more senior position. They could hardly break rules, but had to turn a blind eye to the others, in these dire times.

* *

Ruchi had roses in her cheeks and stars in her eyes. Her parents were delighted at their daughter's obvious happiness. Kavita was thrilled, more because she had predicted this would happen. When Ruchi had mentioned Rajesh, Kavita knew that this dose of sanity was just what her scatterbrained, warm-hearted friend needed.

'Write that story quickly, na, Ruchi', said the ever-focused Kavi. 'It is not like you are marrying tomorrow. And you can buy some sexy stuff, even if you win only 20,000.'

'Where will I wear sexy stuff? We will be living with his parents.'

'Ruch, don't talk like an old maid. You can wear it in your bedroom, for heaven's sake. And on the honeymoon, too. Where is that?'

'Kavi, Mummy and Papa have not even met his parents yet!' Ruchi laughed. 'We are going to Nanded next week.'

Kavita went home feeling very happy for her friend. Unlike Ruchi, she was not especially attractive to boys, or so she thought. She was quite shy; her parents were also quite strict and she seldom met boys outside of church, and she met mainly Christian boys. Not that she minded. She was fine with who she was, and like Ruchi, knew that eventually she would find an old-fashioned steady sort of guy. *One doesn't marry the Sanjays of the world*, she thought. *Though someone will, no doubt*, she added fairly.

She herself was in no hurry to settle down. She had plans. She wanted to be a columnist for a newspaper or a magazine. After a few years' experience, maybe she would be a columnist for several publications. In time to come she might start her own publication, or be absorbed by a reputed house. The latter was more in her line, and to this end, she went about garnering experience. She was already blogging. Her blog underindiansky.blogspot.com was starting to get many visitors. She discussed anything and everything that her generation could possibly be interested in.

Kavita expected the Indus story to help her meet more writers. She was not looking at Rs. 2 lakh. She was aiming for Rs 20,000. It was enough to get her to meet people. Several subjects for a story had suggested themselves to her. She had grown up with her Cinderellas and Red Riding Hoods, Enid Blytons, and then came Harry Potter. It opened magical doors and Kavita daydreamed about witches and wizards appearing in the Vashi market the way Ruchi dreamt of boys. What if the buses coming out of Vashi bus stand became invisible hovercrafts? What if all vehicles were invisible once running and then suddenly became visible if they crossed the speed limit? What if St Agnes's was a boarding school? What if she became Ruchi and Ruchi became her? These were the questions little Kavita had pondered for years, on her way back home from school. These what ifs were definitely going to be the substance of her story. She hoped it would not come out too childish.

* *

The Beauty and the Beast

By Kavita D'Sa

Angie Bull sat fat and beggarly at the entrance to the school, scaring the little girls and boys as they went in. She did not move or even speak. She simply sat and they were scared. She was there when they arrived at school each morning, and she was there when they left each afternoon. The more daring children sometimes went within touching distance, but did not actually touch her.

A nun would come out each morning at 8 a.m. and give her some bread and butter. At 1 p.m., she would get a bowl of dal and rice, which she devoured greedily, and handed the empty bowl back to the impatient ayah who had brought it to her. She probably got something at night as well; no one knew. No one knew who she was, where she had come from, or even how old she was. She could have been anything from 35 to 50 years of age.

One day there was a crowd around Angie Bull. 'Go, children, go to assembly.' Sister Margaret shooed away the more inquisitive children. 'Angie Bull's done pee-pee', 'Angie Bull's had a baby', and 'Angie Bull's dead' were the rumours that these rumour-mongers circulated in school. The last was actually true. Angie Bull had died, perhaps the night before. When Sister Margaret had gone to give her some bread and butter, she had found her laid out stiff.

The good nuns who fed her and sheltered her on their verandah called the police and the doctor. If the old man in the crowd had not recognized her as a prostitute from Kamathipura, the red-light district of Mumbai, they would never have traced her to her native Mahur. They went through her belongings—a dirty white cloth bundle. Apart from a few odd bits of cloth, there was an old-fashioned steel box, a small, round one that she could cup in her palms. It had a thin, broken gold chain and a letter.

* *

Angie Bull's brother turned out to be a handsome, not yet middle-aged man, weather-beaten by life. He recounted how his beautiful young sister had fled the village with the man she loved. The parents, naturally, had been devastated. But they did not know where to trace her. They had lodged a police complaint. Then for years, they made the weekly trip to the men in khaki, in the hope of some news. The brother, Manohar, seldom left the village, for he was a farmer.

He had been 16 when his sister left, now he was 33. That would make her 35 or 36. Not so old, after all. Seventeen years softens memories and pain and longing, and he expected that she would return when she did. He was a good man and was shaken by the death of his sister Shewanti. Shewanti Mahurkar— that was Angie Bull's real name. Maybe he was ashamed he had not tried harder, to find her.

* *

Vinayak's death left Shewanti dazed. That one night of bliss and a bloody knifing later, she was alone. The looks on the faces of the men around her left her in doubt about what was about to happen to her. She screamed and screamed. No one heard.

* *

Shewanti was pretty, really pretty, and docile. She barely spoke and everyone thought it was because she was docile. She gave her body and quietly accepted the money she got in return. She did not know what else to do. No one knew that the madness was slowly eating away into her until one day she calmly bludgeoned a client and walked away into the night.

* *

The fat woman outside St Agnes's was terrifying passersby. She stood in the middle of the pavement and lunged at them. But she did not lunge at Sister Margaret. And when led inside the compound, she went meekly. The lunging attacks continued for a few years, which earned her the nickname of Angie Bull. And then she went quiet again and after a few years, died, just as quiet.

* *

Kavita studied the outline of her story several times. Angie Bull had been a fixture outside St Agnes's, but the rest she had made up. She would have to fill in details. Make it logical. *Why did the nuns not take her to the lunatic asylum? Why give her shelter*? Maybe she needed to change the language. Right now, it read like many other stories she'd read. It smacked too much of the fiction in popular magazines. Moreover, her knowledge of Kamathipura was second-hand. Dare she visit the place? *How do I make it different? And the ending . . . I need some drama.* Three thousand words were not going to be easy.

* *

Kitty Party

by Monica Kapoor

The girls were excited. The 'girls' were four women between the ages of 38 and 46. They had one single thing in common. Or rather two single things. Money. Boredom. Rachita Wadhwa, 38, mother of two. Priyadarshini Mohan, 46, mother of three. Gayatri, 44, childless. Chandni Malhotra, 42, mother of one. This was how the world knew them and this was how they saw themselves. Steeped in domesticity, they had met each other at someone's Dandiya party and got talking. They were all part of one or two other kitty groups, much larger kitty groups where the ladies invited other ladies over mainly to show off crockery, linen, and the culinary skills of their expensive cooks. They talked of clothes and jewellery and then drew the lots, whereby one of them got the kitty that she hardly needed. They were all affluent, affected, and vacant. The 'girls' however, were not vacant, but deeply dissatisfied. They liked each other and decided to start their own little kitty—just for fun. And it was this fun that they were excited about today. The dissatisfaction was forgotten for the day.

They were not meeting at their usual place, but driving out to Madh Island. They booked themselves an air-conditioned Innova and drove out. They intended to wear bikinis and swim at The Retreat, a seaside resort. That is what they had dared each other this month. Rachita and Chandni had lost a few pounds for the occasion; Gayatri was a regular gym enthusiast and always fit. Priyadarshini had struggled but could not shed even a few ounces in anticipation of this big day. She had packed a one-piece as well. They had all gotten a bikini wax—that was also part of the dare.

Monica wondered where her story was headed and if it would pass muster. Her previous epistolary romance had been fun to write. But the word count had been nowhere near 3,000. Plus, her research had been inadequate. She had also not been able to add further twists to the plot, and it felt insipid.

'Must write something from the heart,' she told herself a hundred times.

Mumbai is teeming with stories. Actors, starlets, socialites, beggars, conmen . . .

Which was the world closest to her, the world that she saw the most, the stories that she heard and heard of? She decided to write about that, in the end. At least she would write convincingly! She wrote on.

* *

The rain simply would not stop. And the mobiles were barely functional. All four families had to be informed. They managed that somehow. Rachita's husband was a little put out, but understanding. Gayatri called no one—Rajat was out of town and there was no one else at home. Priyadarshini's husband could barely hear her above the din of the TV, and he mumbled a suitable response, dialled the restaurant downstairs for food. Chandni's phone call ended in tears.

'He doesn't care.' She did not know what was going wrong with her marriage. Neeraj hardly spoke to her, let alone make love. One by one, the little unhappinesses tumbled out. 'He doesn't care what I cook, how I look. He doesn't care if I want to work or don't, he doesn't care how Rishita is doing at school. He just pats her head once every day while she has her dinner. Then he shuts himself in his study. No bedtime stories, no picnics, or outings. Rishita goes with her friend's family to movies and McDonald's. He comes to bed long after I have retired for the night.' Her voice lowered to a whisper: ' . . . hasn't touched or caressed me in an age. Pushes me away when I try to get close. Is he having an affair, I wonder? I think he is having an affair.'

The tears wouldn't stop. 'I am so miserable.' She was blubbering, inconsolable.

* *

Monica did not want her girls to be losers. They were going to find a way out of these daily miseries and rise above themselves. But, how?

* *

Rachita rushed to hug Chandni. Before she realized, she had kissed her. Embarrassed, she pulled back but Chandni wouldn't let go. Gayatri and Priya, stunned at this sudden turn, put out a hand to their friends and found themselves sucked into a tight embrace. The four friends held each other tight. They kissed, they caressed; they erased hurts, disappointments. Hands slid under T-shirts, feeling the still damp bikinis beneath. Bosoms heaved and stomachs tightened with emotion. Tears mingled and wet all their faces.

Then there was calm. They looked at one another, speechless. There was clarity, no embarrassment.

Morning came and they stepped out—head held high, light of step. They drove to Colaba. Had brunch at Café Mondegar. The children would already be at school/college, husbands at work. No need to rush. They savoured their new understanding.

The next month Chandni, Rachita, Gayatri, and Priya met to discuss their new dare. Chandni had confronted her husband. The matter was far less serious than she had imagined. No affair, but an infatuation. They were working on it. It warmed her heart that he felt she was the only person he could talk to. Gayatri and Priya had enrolled for an Art of Living course. Rachita was going to do her MBA the next academic year; meanwhile, she had joined a coaching class nearby. They continued to meet each month with a new dare. But never at Madh Island. They did not need to!

Barely a thousand words. Monica read her story several times and decided she liked it. She was a positive person and did not believe in sad endings. She would figure out what to fit into the story to complete 3,000 words or at least 2,700. Maybe she would add some flirting and diversion at the swimming pool with some men, perhaps foreigners. *Yeah, get some men in. It was too girlie right now.*

* *

Sepoy Govind

By Raghav Singh

A tribute to the late Col. Vikram Singh, a dear friend

Lt. Sandeep Sharma stared unbelievingly at the still-warm body of his dear Govind. There was a gaping hole where his chin had been. The soft, torn flesh hung loose, some of it spattered around. Flecks of skin and muscle were drying on his throat and the shirt was stiffening with the blood that had gushed out of the wound. His .303 lay by his side. It did not need a very intelligent or experienced person to know that Govind had taken his own life.

Sandeep also knew why—it was just that he had thought that Govind was made of sterner stuff. Govind had wanted to go on leave. He was needed badly at his village. The few acres of land that the family owned in their village in Garhwal were being eyed by his cousins. His father, though not very old, had fallen sick. His brother was also in the army and he had taken his family with him for two years. That left only Jamuna his wife and their two sons to look after the old parents, and vice versa. The young and attractive Jamuna, who could also write, had hinted that the cousins were troubling them in more ways than one. She was scared to go out alone. How were they to survive?

Govind had applied for leave; it had even been sanctioned. Then it was cancelled and he was asked to move to the front with the regiment. Sandeep had tried to get the leave sanctioned, had been assured it would happen in a fortnight. They had proceeded northward and moved into the thick of action. When Govind approached the Subedar Major for leave, he was told to wait another fifteen days. Sick with worry, he attended to his 'saab' and his other duties. His wife had begged him to leave everything and come home. He could not dream of deserting. But now he felt he should have deserted while at the base. It was almost impossible to desert from these high mountain passes.

He had given saab his dinner and stepped outside the tent. He hardly realized that he was striding off to the edge of the camp. How the sentry on duty missed him going out of the circle is a mystery. Overcome with despair, cursing his maker and his employers, the man had simply stood under the dark sky and shot himself.

* *

Raghav made outlines for the remainder of his story. It was to be the story of how they could make it look like Govind was killed in the firing action of the night before. His protagonist Sandeep was convinced that Govind was a war casualty. The inability to go to his family in times of need, their torment and his—all this had happened because of the war, so his family should be entitled to his pension. Vikram's copious memoirs had come in really handy here. Raghav was confident of being able to craft an enthralling interrogation sequence. He was also going to plough through the military law and weave a story that used the loopholes in the law that made the dead sepoy eligible for his pension.

After the fat royalty he was receiving for his two self-help books, Raghav was now writing a short story for which he would get a pittance or nothing. But this was liberating, more uplifting than any self-help book he could spin. He set to work; he did not have a lot of time.

* *

On October 9, each editor had a list of twelve names, twelve printed scripts, and two freshly sharpened pencils at his place on the table.

Ramona blessed Meher as she ran her eyes down the list.

1   Lalima, by Maya Sinha

2   Closure, by Jerry Souza

3   The Performance, by Shourya Mehra

4   Maya, by Sanjeevani Iyer

5   Kayuru, by Johny Kutty

6   Sepoy Govind, by Raghav Singh

7   Kitty Party, by Monica Kapoor

8   Beauty and the Beast, by Kavita D'Sa

9   Girl in the Veil, by Rohit Kamra

10 Death by Drowning, by Pallavi Jha

11 Justice, by K. Rajan

12 New Delhi Times, by Paromita Ghosh-Dey

She went through the stories, refreshing them in her mind, as she waited for the others to come in. Today was going to be a long day. It was just five days to the event, and the top six would be informed by mail by midnight. They would all need to book their tickets to Mumbai. The other six would merely be informed that their story had been selected as part of the anthology *Equinox*. The cover design had been selected and the final proofs were at the printers.

Meher, bless her, had the event under control. Banners, props, and other paraphernalia were either already safely in Ramona's office or on their way. Meher's persistent phone calls had ensured that. Their sponsor PrintSoft, a start-up software firm, would be happy. Their flagship product was software for writers, and offices, and this event marketing would help them tremendously. Meher and Ramona had also gone over the itinerary along with Ram Mohan.

The winner and the other five toppers were to report at the Grande Palace by the noon of 14th. Ramona and Meher would have an informal dinner with them at the restaurant downstairs, and brief them about the next day.

On the 15th, they would assemble in the conference hall by 10.30; at 11 a.m. sharp, Sadhana Vaze, Asha

Mahtani, and Vishesh Arora would arrive, the latter two being newly published writers from the Indus stable. They would all share experiences, and Sadhana would be the keynote speaker. It would be an enriching convention followed by a photo session, informal interaction, and lunch, the press note said.

An afternoon tour of Indus House was planned, where the six winners would meet a few local writers who had written for Indus in the past. The four editors who had selected them would also be present, and writing would be discussed. They would be dropped back to the Taj, and they would check out by ten the next day. But that was later.

Now, at Indus conference room, everyone had assembled and the battle began.

'I love the title *Kayuru*. Didn't know Coir is an anglicisation of it.'

'The climax is a little forced . . . I mean . . . the girl trying to strangle him with the coir rope.'

'Why doesn't she really kill him? It's not dramatic enough?'

'It's unusual, and very informative.'

'We are looking at story, not Tell Me Why.'

'Lovely language and flow, though. And structurally sound.'

'Oh, come on! It's fiction. It can have any structure it wants. The question is—is it unputdownable?'

'It shows off Kerala—it is interesting, even if it's not an Aristotelian climax.'

'It is unusual, and beautifully written, these are the plusses—not dramatic enough—these are the minuses, or rather, this is the one minus. Please rank it 1 to 12', Ramona summed it up.

'Hmm . . . Jerry Souza—expected ending, but classical. Appeals to the logic.'

'Too predictable.'

Eventually, Jerry got his votes because of the emotional appeal of the story.

There were verbose opinions for every story. Monica's 'Kitty Party' flowed well; it was stark and real. Everyone knew about the disaffection among the cream of high society; the positive note at the end made it a winner. 'Lalima', made vibrant by colourful street dialogue, addressed a glaring social evil. 'Sepoy Govind' had struck deep; Raghav's brisk prose contrasted sharply with the emotion in the story, making it more poignant, somehow. Kavita D'Sa had taken the editors to a strange land, a place of meeting of the childlike and the wise.

It had taken the editors the complete day to arrive at their decision. The six authors were duly informed.

* *

Rambler had mail. From Indus.

Dear Mr Johny Kutty,

Congratulations! You have won the *first* prize of two lakh rupees for your short story Kayuru. Please make it convenient to attend the award ceremony in Mumbai on October 15, 2013.

We have booked you a suite at the Grande Palace, Colaba. Please check in anytime after 10 a.m. on October 15.

We look forward to interacting and extending our association with you.

Please mail me for any queries.

Warm regards,

Ramona Das

Commissioning Editor

Indus Books Pvt. Ltd.

Well, that was something. Rambler felt a rush. He shared the news with Chettan and Chethathi Amma. 'Why don't you two come with me to Mumbai? It will be a family holiday.'

'What we will do over there, Johny? You go. You will come back here or what?'

'Not sure. If I get an assignment by then, I will go directly there. Or I will travel. Or maybe I'll be in Kerala. See the different cities of Kerala.'

There was an Indigo flight at 8.20 a.m. from Kochi to Mumbai. Rambler booked a taxi to carry him from

Alapuzha to Kochi. They left at 5 in the morning. He reached without mishap and travelled to Mumbai on schedule. He might need to buy himself a decent tie or a suit or something. Well, he could do that in Mumbai. He reached the hotel and was taken into the plush suite he was booked into. He had to share with a Raghav Singh, one of the other five winners of the lesser prize. There were very few single rooms at the hotel and they were booked. Meher had used her contacts at the hotel to get employee discounts for her guests. He messaged Meher to inform her that he'd arrived.

'Welcome. I will meet you all at 6 p.m. in the lobby', she messaged back.

'Will I need a suit for tomorrow?'

'No. Anything formal will do.'

So he could take a gander. He went out to the waterfront. The crème de la crème parked their speedboats and vanity yachts here. They zipped off to Alibagh or someplace else whenever the heat and grime of Mumbai got to them. He walked all over Apollo Bunder and then decided to go to Colaba, as the receptionist at the hotel had told him to. The sun was quite hot and it was really sultry. But he decided to walk anyway. He was still in his travelling clothes—well-worn blue jeans and a shirt. He wasn't too warm. Perhaps he could get a haircut or something.

Colaba was a-teeming with humanity. It was not holiday season yet, nor did he see a lot of tourists. *Gosh, we do have a population.* Well, you should talk, an inner voice told him. Kerala was the most densely populated of all the states in the country.

He ambled into Leopold Cafe. It was a little after noon and he was thirsty. A sinful meal and chilled beer was just what the doctor had ordered. He saw the bullet holes of the infamous November 26 attack of 2008. He remembered that Leopold was the first to come under siege. We forget and move on with our lives. The human brain was programmed for that, true. But to make a celebration of almost anything . . . for months after the attack, people came to Leopold to just gawk at the bullet holes. He took his time over his meal, made conversation with someone with an unpronounceable name and was warned not to buy anything without haggling.

Colaba Causeway was paved with hawkers—bags, shoes, baubles, chappals, curios, nautical compasses and clocks, faux antiques, and even cheaper food for those who could not spend at the cafes. One did not walk on the pavement; one constantly squeezed one's way through. No one seemed to mind that—Mumbai was quite used to her increasing army of people. Rambler bought nothing. He was a smart traveller who carried his souvenirs in his head. On impulse, though, he did turn into a shop selling leather goods. It had been recommended by the man with the unpronounceable name at Leopold—there was a veritable sea of bags and shoes. He bought Kolhapuri chappals for his brother and sister-in-law, and then for himself and Shiny as well. Chethathi had not very small feet, as did Shiny. It was really warm and he took a while walking that half a kilometre back to the hotel.

* *

She could barely contain her excitement. She had practically skipped to work and back. The reason—Indus had called her to Mumbai to receive the Rs. 20,000 prize. And there was the prospect of writing more stories for them. That sounded exciting. Maya had no idea how much money there was in writing regularly, but she could find out. She needed leave from work, from October 13 to October 16, both included. She had decided that she would assess Mr Rajinder's mood. If he appeared happy, she would ask for leave. Otherwise, she would pretend she had fallen ill and just not turn up. *Or manufacture a family emergency—that always works. But he knows I have lost my parents, so what family? What emergency? Hmm . . . let's see.'*

Luck was looking up. Rajinder was elated that a staff member had won a story competition. Not only did he grant her leave, but he also took her picture from the college records, made her write a little piece praising herself and mailed it to his student-customers and every person of importance. He almost gave her a little bonus, but stopped himself in time!

Maya didn't care. She was feeling reckless. She was going shopping. She loved dressing up and it was ages since she had bought herself anything pretty or even moderately priced. Lajpat Nagar. Lovely patiala salwars, vibrant phulkari dupattas, and stylish kurtis—she bought three sets. Her clear skin glowed as she munched chole bhature on the roadside. She was going to look for a pair or two of juttis and then head home. She would book her seat that night. She calculated quickly and decided to treat herself to an AC two-tier seat in the Rajdhani Express.

Train number 12952, Mumbai Rajdhani, New Delhi to Mumbai Central. Departure 16.30, arrival 08.35.

Train number 12951, Mumbai Rajdhani, Mumbai Central to New Delhi. Departure 16.30, arrival 08.35.

Perfect. She booked her departure for the 13th and return for the 16th. She would have to spend a few hours in the waiting room on the 16th, since they had to check out by 10 a.m. She didn't mind that. She might even decide to see something of Mumbai if she found somewhere to keep her suitcase. *Ah . . . let's see.* She went to the neighbour's to get a printout.

She stepped out at Mumbai Central Station and hailed a cab for the Grande Palace. She was a Delhi girl and she knew that distances in Mumbai were vast; nevertheless, the taxi was taking forever to reach, and Rs. 900 seemed a bit much. She got off with the horrible feeling of having been cheated. *Hope the rest of the stay is better than this*, she thought, a little woebegone.

She had messaged her arrival to Meher and received the welcome response and instruction to be in the lobby at 6. *I wonder where the other writers are.* She could hardly go knocking on doors to find out. She did not dare use any of the hotel's services—her budget didn't stretch to spas and salons. She had called Mehjabeen home a day before she travelled to Mumbai and had spent four hours getting the necessary gloss and polish—waxing, facial, manicure, and pedicure. Her hair had recently been cut and styled, so it looked fine.

She looked around, poked around in the wardrobe, gulped when she saw the cost of pressing a single garment printed on the large laundry bag. She helped herself from the platter of fruits, had a long soak in the bathtub. She added a generous amount of bath salts from the white plastic bottle and settled in. Bath over, a refreshing nap later, she was ready for anything. It was only just 4 p.m. Sensibly, she had shaken out and hung up her dresses. She made herself a cup of tea and ate some biscuits. There was no one really whom she could call and share her excitement. She'd call Neha, she decided.

'Hey, Neha, I am in Mumbai.'

'Really? Why?'

'You won't believe this, but—'

'Maya, sweetie, I'll call you later—' Neha said and Maya could hear the wail of Neha's younger one, a child of six. She watched TV. At precisely a quarter to six, she made her way to the lift, looking gorgeous in a deep pink and turquoise combination.

* *

'October 15, 2013', he read off his mail. 'Now they tell me! I have just four days in which to make arrangements and move to Mumbai. From Mussoorie. Have they any idea?' Under his breath, he hurled an expletive at the unknown executive of Indus Books. Raghav was unsurprised at being awarded a prize for his story. What surprised him was that they had not seen fit to award him the first prize of two lakh rupees. The story was compelling, he knew that. His writing experience had told him he could grab eyeballs. But that should not make him arrogant. Maybe the better writer won. He was just glad that his tribute to Vikram would not go unnoticed. He had grown really fond of the old man during their brief association. They were both lonely souls and had connected well. There was deep understanding yet no intrusion. They had enjoyed each other's company. The ships had passed. And now he was alone. *Thank God he died peacefully in his sleep, in his own home.*

Life goes on.

Mumbai would be a good interlude before he came back and started working on his next book. He would stop over in Delhi and catch up with a few friends too.

Train number 12952, Mumbai Rajdhani, New Delhi to Mumbai Central. Departure 16.30, arrival 08.35.

Train number 12951, Mumbai Rajdhani, Mumbai Central to New Delhi. Departure 16.30, arrival 08.35.

Perfect. Raghav booked for the 13th from Delhi and the 16th from Mumbai.

He would leave Mussoorie on the 12th, early. Reach Delhi by late afternoon or early evening. His sturdy Wagon R had recently been serviced; it would take him through. He called Sunil to let him know that he would need to leave the car with him. 'No problem, yaar' was the answer, as Raghav had expected. Now he needed to get his clothes sorted.

The mail had said 'Dress: Formal. Mumbai would be warm, so he could dispense with a blazer. But he might just need one for his few evenings in Delhi, later. He did not have a huge wardrobe, so he simply took one of the lighter suits. He hung it in a suit cover in his car and drove off to Delhi. He enjoyed his driving. Raghav was singing with his music system, as he went along. Old Hindi film songs sung by Kishore Kumar, were quite his favourite. A quick stop at a dhaba for a rajma-chawal and he was off again. He spent a pleasant evening with Sunil, reminiscing about their IIM days. Sunil was steadily climbing the ladder, but Raghav could no longer be seduced by corporate success.

The journey to Mumbai was uneventful and he was deposited at the hotel and thence to his room. He realized he had been conned by prepaid taxi; it had not been a legal thing at all. Living in Mussoorie, he really was unused to the thugs of the metropolises.

He had a few hours before he met the others at six in the lounge. He had dealt with Indus publishers entirely via mail and did not know Meher who had sent him the welcome SMS and asked him to be in the lounge at six. Meanwhile, a quick lunch and then a good sleep was just what the doctor ordered. Thusly refreshed, he went down for a swim.

I could get used to the good life. He smiled at his reflection in the mirror. He combed back his hair neatly and went down to meet the other writers.

* *

Kavita broke the ice. Her mother had expressed her reservations about her being alone in the hotel room, but Kavita was adamant. 'Mummy, are you going to travel with me when I start working or what? And it's in Mumbai only.' Mrs D'Sa had conceded the logic.

'I am here for the Equinox event', she said to the few other people who were in the lobby at a quarter to six, clearly waiting for someone.

Rambler and Raghav, already in conversation, turned around. Her heart skipped a beat when Rambler smiled through his newly trimmed beard. Maya turned around as well and this time Raghav's heart skipped a beat.

Ramona and Meher walked in. 'I see you all already know one another.'

'So, *Kayuru*, huh? It held us spellbound, I must tell you.'

'All the stories did'.

'Raghav, we have published you before, haven't we? I wasn't with Indus then.'

'I am really looking forward to seeing Indus House. I want to see the inside of a publishing house. I have chosen writing as a career, you see.' This from the confident young Kavita.

'I was just so glad my Lalima was selected. It took forever to weave the plot. I must have changed it at least three times.'

Lovely voice, too, Raghav thought. He moved forward. 'Where do you live, Maya?'

Everyone was talking all at once.

'Kerala is a very interesting place these days . . .'

'Writing for magazines, maybe I will start there . . .'

'Defence colony . . .'

'I visit Delhi often . . .'

'OK, folks', Meher interrupted the babble. 'Monica is on her way, delayed by the Mumbai traffic . . . oh . . . oh, that could be her.'

Monica, elegant as ever in a pair of maroon trousers and floral kurti, smiled at the group. There was a fresh round of introductions.

'And Jerry and Maria Souza have been delayed on the expressway, so they will join us directly at the Thai restaurant here', Meher continued, like she had never been interrupted.

'No, I am not staying here, I live so close by; it would be ridiculous', Monica informed Maya, as they all walked around, admiring the property. You could feel the century-old history here. They would head to the bar in about 20 minutes. They had all agreed that they would pay for their own drinks and dinner would be on Indus. Maya worried about the price again. She did not really want to drink, but she did so want to belong. Even a soft drink would cost the earth, she was sure. She sighed. A large part of her 20,000 would vanish right here, tonight, it seemed. *Oh, forget it. I'll just have fun.* Raghav seemed more than ordinarily interested in her, she thought.

Over drinks, Rambler regaled them with delightful travel tales from all over the world. The whiskeys had warmed them all up nicely. Only Maya and Kavita were sipping cautiously at their margaritas. Maya felt Raghav's eyes on her several times. She looked up. Monica had noticed it too. The women smiled in mutual understanding. Everyone, it seemed, had let down their guards. Everyone, it seemed, needed someone.

They trooped into the Red Dragon for a seafood meal but ended up ordering the Peking duck and crisp lamb with dimsums. The Souzas joined them there. They got into a wangle with Rambler about Goa versus Kerala as a holiday destination.

'Goa is getting unsafe. It's a drug haven', Rambler was saying and Jerry had to agree.

'Next holiday, Kerala,' Maria promised Rambler.

'The submission process *is* that long, Kavita. There is nothing you can do about it.'

'Yes, but suppose it is something completely different, way out?'

'Even then.' Meher smiled at the enthusiastic young girl.

Meher was good naturedly answering Kavita's bombarding. Ramona was holding forth with Maya, Raghav, and Monica.

'Everyone is writing and everyone is getting published. The competition is huge, for writers and for publishers. And we have to look for writing for other media as well. Sadhana Vaze will tell you a lot more about this tomorrow.'

Dessert was over—the unanimous favourite, caramel custard. She caught Meher's eye.

'Right, everyone. Shall we call it a day? It's been a long day for all of you. We meet at the Blue Room tomorrow at ten. Oh and there's been a change in plan. We will not be going back to Indus House. We figured that travelling would take up a lot of time.'

'Don't worry, Indus House will come here to you.' She smiled at Kavita's crestfallen face.

* *

The Blue Room was buzzing. Rohan Bagade and another office boy from Indus were overseeing the arrangements—chairs, podium, etc. Meher, with the help of a technician, was running the Indus House film in a loop. It was to Jay Kapoor's credit that Indus House, unceremoniously sandwiched between two commercial complexes in Andheri, looked stately and impressive in the film. The 15-minute film ended spectacularly with books spilling on the screen, happy smiling authors' faces, and dollar notes popping up. It ended with a bold 'India Writes for Indus' flashing across the screen.

Monica arrived early, cool and elegant in a pearl-pink trouser suit, and took her designated chair. Rambler, Raghav, and Jerry had been for a swim in the morning. The women had relaxed and taken their time to dress up. Kavita wore a chiffon sari with a braouse, both a dusty pink. Her mother had been shocked, but here Ruchi had stepped in. 'Aunty, please, let her, all decent people also wear these blouses these days.' Kavita's mother had finally acceded. Kavita accessorized only with earrings, hair tumbling about her in the just-out-of-bed look favoured by the young girls these days. Maria wore a black silk dress. Maya shone resplendent in a haldi-kumkum patiala salwar and kurti. Kohl-lined eyes and nude lipstick, freshly shampooed and conditioned hair left to cascade gorgeously around her head and shoulders completed the charming picture.

There was tea and coffee and biscuits for those who wanted it. They all settled down. Sadhana, Vishesh, and Asha arrived and took their seats. The chief guest was a member from the Jaykar family—a prominent name in Mumbai academic and literary circles. It would guarantee good press coverage, Ramona had surmised, and she was right. She welcomed the guests and made a short inaugural address.

'Reading, and therefore, writing will never go out of fashion. What is hugely encouraging is that more and more people are attempting it these days—it is no longer something out there that only a select few can access or attempt. Indus takes it upon itself to attract and encourage new talent. Please get it straight from the horses' mouths, our latest new writers—Vishesh Arora and Asha Mahtani.'

Vishesh spoke about travel writing. He had travelled on foot through many states in India and spoke endearingly of the stories he'd encountered—a man who had vowed to talk to 10,000 people, the dhaba owners from Punjab, the man who walked backwards all the way from his home in Tamilnadu to the Ayyappa temple at Sabarimala, the highway vendors who popped up with fresh produce and disappeared like magic—there was a fascinating tale behind everything ordinary. 'Man is kind, mankind is cruel. Travel reaffirmed my faith in people.' Vishesh ended his talk.

Asha talked about Agatha Christie, her idol. 'I revised my book 17 times before I sent it to Indus', she said of her maiden publication.

Sadhana was introduced as the keynote speaker and when she rose to speak, there was a small applause from the six writers who had seen her video. She recounted how she had created her favourite story, 'The Gas Man'. 'Every summer, we would meet at my grandparents' house in Konkan. All eight cousins. We told each other ghost stories after dusk. We all saw shapes on floors or walls. My brother would see shapes in the air. That was the birth of 'The Gas Man', the lovable apparition who scared no one. I loved creating his laugh-out loud attempts at appearing fearsome to a gang of boisterous tweens. Children get a kick out of out-smarting ghosts. Funny stories are good fun. But there's nothing funny about how much you have to work at it!' she ended passionately, as the audience tittered.

The chief guest congratulated all the winners and gave away the awards. Rambler, as winner of the first prize, was asked to say a few words. 'Writing cannot happen without passion. It's not only about the money, although I won't say *no* to this!' He laughed as he patted the pocket of his shirt where he had deposited his cheque.

Equinox was officially launched.

* *

There was lunch, tasty Indian fare. The entire Indus gang had descended and Monica was pleased to see that Geeta remembered her from the Lit Club meeting. Vidya and Maya discussed children's literature. 'My son hardly reads. I don't know what books there are that he will like.' Vidya gave her several names—Leela Broome, Arifa Tehsin—there were fascinating tales of nature and of animals, for children. 'If you choose to continue writing, and want us to publish, Maya, route your work through our website.'

The Souzas left immediately after lunch. They had to drive back to Pune; their truck could arrive any time. Kavita and Monica offered to show the others around Mumbai. 'Or you could all come over to my place and we could chill.' Finally, they decided to get into comfortable clothes and walk. Monica's high heels would not permit that, so she bade everyone a warm goodbye and went home. Kavita, Rambler, Maya, and Raghav went to the Gateway of India, took a boat ride. They visited the Jehangir Art Gallery and the Sassoon Library—*we could have had the event here*, Maya thought.

They returned to the hotel only after dinner. Rambler and Kavita said goodbye; they would both leave early in the morning. Raghav and Maya were both booked on the Rajdhani, in the evening, and they decided to travel together. Raghav had friends to visit, Maya had none.

He preferred to wait with her at the railway waiting room.

'It's good we travelled together this time. I was cheated on my way to the hotel.'

'Join the club', Raghav laughed.

They discovered they were in the same club for a number of other things—they both loved the unrelenting beauty of the mountains, both were fascinated with the idea of writing as a career, both were divorced.

Raghav was a pleasant travel companion. They had seats in the same bogie and spent a good amount of time with each other.

'*Kulladwali chai.*' Raghav handed her the earthen cup brimming with hot, spiced tea. '*Special banwai.*' Maya was touched that he had thought to have it specially brewed. She knew he was trying to impress her, and she was enjoying that.

By the time they reached Delhi they knew a little bit about each other. Maya loved Vikram's life story and the picture of Mussoorie that Raghav created for her. 'October is a flower fest. Come over.'

Raghav could not stop laughing at her accounts of Rajinder College, government-unrecognised.

'I think I can write a book on the education tamasha now', Maya declared, flushed from the warmth of good interaction.

When they ended their journey at Delhi, Raghav took Maya's hand and said, 'Come to Mussoorie.'

His eyes said, 'Come to me.'

Maya's eyes met his. 'I will', she said, and meant it.

* *

Rambler reached Alapuzha. He spent some time regaling Chethathi Amma with stories about Mumbai. She loved the kolhapuri chappals. 'But your Chettan . . . he likes his black leather slippers only . . .'

As soon as was decently possible, he headed for Shiny's coir workshop. He spoke to Sivadasan, told him about the money he had and they discussed what best could be done with it. Sivadasan spoke at length while Rambler used every bit of self-control not to tap impatiently on the desk. Finally, the scent of flowers announced the arrival of Shiny. She came in and he gave her the Kolhapuri chappals and a copy of *Equinox* (all the authors had received two copies). She smiled and said nothing. A feeling he had not felt before welled up in him. He could not describe it and it annoyed him. 'Bye', he said and started walking away.

'Hey!' He turned back at Shiny's call. She was standing, hands on hips. She was wearing the chappals and smiling broadly. She winked.

The leaves were greener, the breeze cooler, and birdsong sweeter. The sun was pure gold.

He grinned and walked back to her. Life was looking up!

* *